W9-DES-318

A PLACE CALLED HOME

This Large Print Book carries the
Seal of Approval of N.A.V.H.

NEW MEXICO, BOOK 2

30036010089595

A PLACE CALLED HOME

HEARTBREAK OF THE PAST
DRAWS A COUPLE TOGETHER
IN THIS HISTORICAL NOVEL

JANET LEE BARTON

THORNDIKE PRESS
A part of Gale, Cengage Learning

GALE
CENGAGE Learning™

Detroit • New York • San Francisco • New Haven, Conn • Waterville, Maine • London

GALE
CENGAGE Learning™

LIBRARY OF CONGRESS CATALOGING-IN-PUBLICATION DATA

Barton, Janet Lee.
    A place called home : heartbreak of the past draws a couple together in this historical novel / by Janet Lee Barton.
        p. cm. — (Thorndike Press large print christian fiction)
    (New Mexico ; bk. 2)
    ISBN-13: 978-1-4104-1173-0 (alk. paper)
    ISBN-10: 1-4104-1173-7 (alk. paper)
    1. New Mexico—Fiction. 2. Large type books. I. Title.
PS3602.A84228P54 2009
813'.6—dc22   2008039266

Published in 2009 by arrangement with Barbour Publishing, Inc.

To my Lord and Savior for showing me the way.
I thank Him for the family I was born into, for the family He's given me, and for my parents, William B. (Red) and Thelma Heaton, who faithfully instilled a deep abiding love of the Lord in us all and who encouraged my love of reading and writing always. What a blessing to know that one day I'll see them again in their "place called home" in heaven.

CHAPTER 1

1898 — Roswell, New Mexico Territory
Beth Morgan looked at the clock on the wall beside the switchboard. One thirty. She inserted the pin into Alma Burton's line's socket and pulled the lever for two rings. She pulled the lever again.

"Yes?" asked a sleepy-sounding Alma.

"Mrs. Alma, you wanted me to let you know when it was time to take your cake out of the oven," Beth reminded her. It wasn't unusual for her to serve as a kitchen timer a couple of times a day — especially for some of the older women in the community.

"Oh, thank you, dear. I would have plumb forgotten if you hadn't reminded me." Alma sounded more awake now.

"You are very welcome. You have a good day." Beth felt all but certain Mrs. Burton had been napping when she rang her. She pulled the pin out of the socket and chuckled. She still couldn't get over how very different being a telephone operator for the Roswell Telephone and Manufacturing Company was from the Bell Telephone Company where she'd received her training back East. There had been so many rules and regulations — the primary one being not to talk to the customers. Those rules never made it out to New Mexico Territory, and for that she was very thankful. Otherwise, she'd be in big trouble with the superintendent. Most of the telephone customers thought of the operators as their own personal message service.

The light over the sheriff's office line lit up. Beth connected the line pin. "Number, please."

"Beth? Is that you?"

Her heart skittered in her chest as she recognized Deputy Matt Johnson's voice. "Yes, it's me, Matt."

"We've heard from Jeb Winslow. He's on his way to Roswell."

Her heart sank. "When will he be here?"

"He was up in Colorado when he got the letter. He's on his way now. Sheriff and I figure he'll get to town sometime in the next week or so."

Beth nodded but couldn't speak.

"I'm sorry, Beth. I think we've all been

8

hoping he wouldn't be found."

She swallowed around the knot of unshed tears in her throat. "Yes, well, thank you for letting me know, Matt."

Beth pulled the pin from the socket without waiting on a reply from the deputy. Her worst fear had just been realized. How was she going to let Cassie and Lucas go? They didn't even know their uncle. She was glad Jessica was busy at the other switchboard and hoped she couldn't tell how upset she was at the news she'd just heard.

Laura Brewster's light came on above her socket.

"Number, please?"

"Doc Bradshaw, please."

Beth connected the two lines and watched the light go out over both Doc's and Laura's sockets, letting her know she'd made a successful connection. She fought back the tears that threatened and glanced at the clock again. Her friend and coworker, Darcie Malone, would be relieving her soon, then she could leave. Most of the time she was thankful for her job as telephone operator at the Roswell Telephone and Manufacturing Company, but today she just wanted to get home. She needed to figure out what to say to Harland's children. She didn't quite know how to tell them their uncle had been found and was on his way to claim them.

It'd been only two months since their father and her fiancé had died in a cattle stampede, but she'd come to love Cassie and Lucas. And she didn't like the idea of giving them up to a man they didn't know, even if he was their uncle.

The lights came on again first over Laura's socket and then Doc's, alerting her that their conversation was over. She unplugged each socket. While Beth knew most of what went on in Roswell because of her job and the fact that everyone seemed to think she should or did know their business, she tried not to listen in on conversations — something the superintendent, Mr. McQuillen, was still working on with Darcie.

The light under the Roswell Hotel socket lit up, and she plugged the pin into it. "Number, please."

"Get me the sheriff's office, please, Beth," Morris Benson, the hotel clerk, requested.

Beth plugged the other pin into the socket of the sheriff's office and pulled the lever to ring their phone. She then made sure the lights went off before she answered the next call.

When Mr. Church, the general manager, and Mr. McQuillen had started the Roswell

Telephone and Manufacturing Company in 1894, there were only thirty-five subscribers. Beth had been one of the first two operators hired, after her ailing aunt, whom she'd come out West to care for, had passed away. The company had grown considerably since it started, and now there were six regular operators and one relief . . . and about four installers who put up the lines and ran them into customers' homes. Nearby farms and ranches were being serviced now, and long distance to Eddy would be coming in the next year or so. No telling how many more employees there would be in the coming years.

She couldn't help but wonder if she'd still be here, if her life kept changing as much as it had in the past year. So much had happened. It was hard enough to believe she'd answered an advertisement for a mail-order bride as a dare, much less that she'd ended up accepting the proposal of the man who'd written back, even before he decided to join her out West in Roswell and start their life together.

He'd bought a piece of land, sight unseen, to start a small ranch and had planned on courting her proper while he got his herd started and refurbished the house on the land. Then they'd get married.

11

Barely a month after he arrived, Harland had been out working with the small herd of cattle he'd bought for the ranch when a dry lightning storm blew up. Evidently, from what one of the neighbors had said, a bolt struck close and frightened the cattle. Harland had been caught in the ensuing stampede. Just thinking about it made her shudder. She was so relieved the children had been staying in town with her until Harland was able to fix up the house and hadn't been there to see the death of their father.

Beth still couldn't quite believe it all. Feeling that it was her fault, she'd wished over and over again that she'd never answered that advertisement . . . believing that if Harland hadn't come out here, he'd still be alive. Now it seemed there was more heartache in store — if she had to give up the children she'd come to love.

Darcie showed up to relieve her, right on time, and Beth relinquished her spot in front of the switchboard quickly, as they'd been trained to do. Darcie immediately slipped into the chair right behind her and began connecting two lit-up sockets.

"Beth, what's wrong?" Darcie called as Beth pulled on the shawl she'd worn to work and started out the door.

"Oh, Darcie, I'm sorry." Beth turned back

12

to her friend, realizing how rude she must have appeared, heading out the door without so much as a nod to her. She tried to keep her voice low so the whole office wouldn't know her business, but she knew it was only a matter of time until they did. "I'm not thinking straight. Harland's brother has been found, and Deputy Matt says he'll be here to collect the children in about a week. I just don't know how I'll be able to let them go."

Darcie jumped up and hugged her. "Oh, Beth, I'm so sorry I dared you to answer that advertisement for a mail-order bride. It's my fault you are so unhappy now."

Beth shook her head. "No, Darcie, it's not your fault. It's my own impulsiveness that caused my problem. I'd always wondered what it would be like to answer one of those advertisements. It was Harland's sweet letters that made me begin to care for him and accept his offer of marriage. And I feel to blame. If I hadn't accepted his proposal, and if he hadn't come out here and been caught in that stampede —"

"You'd be a happily married woman by now, instead of having two children to care for alone. Harland's death was not your fault, Beth." The switchboard lit up in several places, and Darcie slid back into the chair and hurriedly disconnected two parties and connected two others.

Beth sighed. Maybe it wasn't all her fault . . . but she wasn't sure Darcie's picture of the future would have been true. She'd been having second thoughts about marrying Harland and had been trying to figure out what to do about it before he died. Now she was just thankful that he hadn't known. She'd been terribly confused about so many things lately, but one thing was for certain, she didn't regret offering to keep his children. Not for one moment.

Lines unlit for the time being, Darcie turned back to her. "It might be for the best, you know, Beth."

Beth did know many in town would think that. All her friends thought she was a little daft for taking in Harland's children. Well, not Emma and Deputy Matt or Cal and Liddy McAllister. They had been very supportive of her, and she was thankful for that.

And she was blessed that she had a home to offer the children. Thankfully, they'd been living with her in the small house she'd inherited from her aunt Gertrude, so there was no need to uproot them after their father's death. She didn't make a lot of money, but the Lord would provide for them. Of that, Beth had no doubt. She'd taken them in, presumably, until Harland's brother could be found, but she didn't really think he would be, and she'd truly hoped he wouldn't. Now she had to face the fact that Lucas and Cassie's uncle at least cared enough to come and see his niece and nephew. She would continue to hope that Jeb Winslow would let her have custody of Harland's children. From what Harland had told her about his brother, he wasn't the settling-down kind. She was going to hold out hope that maybe, just maybe, he'd be glad to let them stay with her.

"It will all work out, Beth." Darcie tried to reassure her again.

Beth nodded. "Well, it's all in the Lord's hands now, but I sure hope Mr. Winslow doesn't take them far away. Maybe he'll decide to stay. Mr. Myers, Harland's lawyer, said he'd talked to him about making out a new will, but of course he hadn't had a chance to get to it with so much to do. His old will appointed Jeb Winslow as the children's guardian. They inherit the land, but he has the say so as to whether to sell it or keep it for them. I hope he'll settle here so at least I can keep watch over them."

The switchboard lit up again, and Beth was relieved not to have to keep talking about it. She waved good-bye and hurried

15

out the door.

Jeb dismounted his horse and tied it at the hitching post just outside the cemetery gate, his heart still aching. He'd been riding for several weeks — ever since he received the letter telling him that his brother had died in a stampede, leaving two orphaned children behind. He'd come to take on the responsibility of raising them, even though the very thought of it scared him more than coming face-to-face with a mother bear. *Dear Lord, please help me to do it right. You know I know nothing about bringing up children, so I'm just going to look to You to help me.*

He thought about his niece and nephew. Last time he saw them, Cassie was about four or five, and Lucas was a toddler. Now they'd be about nine and six . . . ten and seven? He didn't know. Remorse flooded Jeb's soul. Why hadn't he visited them more often? But no. He'd always had other things to do, other places to go. Why, he hadn't even known Mary died or that Harland had decided to move out West until he got the letter telling him his brother had died. Jeb figured the Lord must have been guiding that letter through the mail for him to have gotten it at all. It had been to the last two places he'd worked before the post ever made it to him.

He'd only been working at this last ranch up in southern Colorado for little over a year — and that was long for him. His boss had been hinting about making him a foreman, and he was seriously thinking it might be time to settle down. He sure wasn't getting any younger; he still limped from the last time he'd been thrown trying to break a horse, and he didn't seem to be getting any better.

Dry grass crackled under his boots until he found the spot he was looking for. Taking off his hat, he knelt down and blinked through the sudden tears that formed on seeing the gravestone bearing his brother's name. Childhood memories came flooding back as he remembered the laughing, teasing, and fighting they'd done in their youth. His timing sure was bad. How he wished he'd gone home for one last visit. But all the wishing in the world couldn't undo the past.

He swallowed around the lump in his throat and stood. All he could do now for his brother was to raise his children the best he could. Taking a deep breath, Jeb set his hat on his head and took long strides back to his horse. He mounted and turned toward the main street of Roswell. He had to find his niece and nephew. They were the only family he had left.

On the outskirts of town, he noticed a cluster of nice new buildings on North Hill. He'd heard the New Mexico Military Institute had reopened in a new spot just this year, and sure enough, the sign outside the main building proved it hadn't been rumor after all. Funding had closed it down for several years, but he'd seen in a paper where it had been slated to open this very month.

As he rode into town and down Main Street, Jeb couldn't help but notice how much Roswell had grown since he'd last been through about three years ago. There were four or five large hotels, four mercantile houses, several drugstores, three blacksmith shops, two livery stables, three barbers, cafés, a bakery, a lumberyard, a telephone office — all kinds of new businesses that weren't here last time he'd been through. It was now a bustling, thriving town. He reined in and hitched his horse outside the sheriff's office and went inside.

A man about his age looked up from his desk and stood when Jeb walked toward him. "Howdy. I'm Deputy Matt Johnson. What can I do for you?"

Jeb nodded. "Afternoon, Deputy. I'm Jeb

Winslow, and I need to know where my brother's children are."

"We've been expecting you, Mr. Winslow." The deputy stood up and extended his hand. He motioned to the chair in front of the desk. "Have a seat. I'm sure sorry about the loss of your brother. It was an awful accident."

Jeb shook the deputy's hand and lowered himself into the chair. He nodded and cleared his throat, suddenly finding it hard to speak.

The deputy crossed the room and poured a cup of coffee from the pot on the stove sitting in the middle of the room. He brought it over and handed it to him.

Jeb took a drink and swallowed. "Thank you. Road's been dry," he commented, but he had a feeling the deputy knew the dust had nothing to do with his hoarseness. "Can you tell me exactly what happened? How did my brother get caught up in a stampede?"

"Best we can figure, a bolt of lightning spooked his cattle, and he just got caught in the middle." He paused. "Did your brother have much experience ranching?"

Jeb shook his head. "Not that I know of. Harland was a farmer back home, but we hadn't seen each other in a long time. Still,

I don't know that he ever owned a herd of cattle."

The deputy nodded. "Some of the neighbors said he seemed a little green."

"Might have been." Jeb had seen stampedes before, and the very thought of his brother dying in one still sickened him. He could barely think it, much less say it, but he had to ask. "Did the children see —"

"No, thank the Lord. They were in town."

Jeb sighed with relief and nodded. He gazed out the window a moment before speaking. "Can you tell me where they are now?"

"They're in very good hands. Harland's fiancée, Beth Morgan, has been taking real good care of them." The deputy ambled to the door and motioned to a building down a ways on the other side of the street. It bore a sign bearing the name, THE ROSWELL TELEPHONE AND MANUFACTURING COMPANY, and Jeb remembered passing it on the way there.

Deputy Johnson continued. "Beth works across the street as a telephone operator and lives in a house a few blocks away. She should be getting off work soon, but the children will be in school for another couple of hours."

Jeb let out a deep breath. "That'll give me

time to clean up before I see them." He brushed at the travel dust on his pants. "I wouldn't want to scare them at first sight."

The deputy chuckled. "Probably wouldn't hurt to spruce up some. But Lucas and Cassie are good children with nice manners. They'd never mention that thick layer of dust you've collected getting here to them."

"Thank you for your help, Deputy. I'm sure I'll be seeing you."

"The lawyer who handled your brother's will has an office over on Third Street, going west. It's about two blocks down. His name is John Myers," Matt informed him. "Harland got a good deal on the land. It's not a big ranch, but it's a prime location, just outside of town. But the house is in pretty bad shape. If you are going to stay, you'll want to do some repairs. You might consider leaving the children with Beth until it's livable."

Jeb hadn't even thought that far ahead. He just wanted his brother's children to know they had some kin left in the world. He needed to ride out to the ranch his brother owned and see how much work was needed to get the house habitable . . . and he'd better visit that lawyer and tie up any loose ends. But all that could wait. Right now he needed to board his horse at a livery stable and find a hotel room. After a bath, he'd go meet his niece and nephew. "Thanks, Deputy. I appreciate your advice. I'll think on it."

"Come on back when you're ready, and I'll take you to see the children."

Jeb nodded. "Thank you. I think I'll take you up on that offer."

Beth Morgan was on her way home from the telephone office. It'd been over a week since Matt had told her Jeb Winslow was on his way to Roswell. That was probably what drew her gaze to the sheriff's office across the street. But it was the sight of a tall, broad-shouldered cowboy coming out of the office that had her heart hammering in her chest. He walked with a slight limp and was larger than Harland, but there was something about him. . . .

He glanced her way and tipped his hat. For a minute she held her breath, wondering if he was Jeb Winslow, come to get the children. But when he headed down the other side of the street, she breathed a sigh of relief and hurried home.

Ever since Matt had told her Jeb was on his way back, she'd been meeting each day with a feeling of dread. She didn't want him to come after his niece and nephew, and she was aware she was being very selfish. She just couldn't help it. She wanted to raise them. From all she'd heard from Harland, Jeb Winslow was the last person who should have them. Harland had mentioned more than once how he wished his younger brother would settle down and how disappointed he was that he'd never been able to convince him to do so.

She went to the kitchen and put on the teakettle, disconcerted at how shaky she was at seeing the stranger coming out of the sheriff's office. Like it or not, Lucas and Cassie's uncle would be here before too long, and she was going to have to give them up. But however was she going to be able to do that? They didn't even know the man! Surely he wouldn't just come and get them and leave. She bowed her head.

Dear Lord, please help me to accept Your will in this. I know I'm not blood kin, but I love Cassie and Lucas, and they know me. I can't bear the thought of them moving away with a stranger, even if he is the only family they have left in the world. Please keep them here. In Jesus' name I pray, amen.

There was nothing more to do. She needed to leave it in the Lord's hands. The kettle began to whistle, and she made herself a cup of tea. Maybe it would soothe her frazzled nerves. She'd drink it, then go to meet the children at the Third Street School.

She'd taken to going to the school and walking home with them ever since Harland's death. Both children were still grieving. She knew they were. Yet they seldom let her see their tears, and that made her want to cry for them. Today, they seemed in good spirits when they came running out the door.

It was a crisp September day with brilliant blue skies and a light breeze that sent the cottonwood leaves swirling around their feet while they strolled home. Lucas kicked at the leaves as Cassie told Beth about their day, and both children were full of excitement about the upcoming fair at the beginning of October.

"Grace says they build a palace out of bales of alfalfa and have the exhibits in it. She says it is huge!" Lucas said excitedly.

Beth grinned at his little-boy enthusiasm. "It's called an alfalfa palace and, yes, they do have exhibits in it."

"I can't wait to see it." Lucas skipped a few paces ahead.

Cassie laughed. "That's all he's been talking about, Miss Beth."

"Well, we'll be sure to go, so he'll get to

24

see it for real. The McAllisters are sure to have some exhibits. I wouldn't mind entering a few things. Aunt Gertrude's receipt for apple pie is hard to beat."

"Oh, that would be great fun!" Cassie exclaimed. "May we help?"

"Of course you can help. Maybe we'll make some jam, too." They were near home, and Beth watched Lucas run around a tree and dart ahead before coming to a sudden stop. She glanced past him to the front stoop of her home. Deputy Matt stood there with the man she'd seen coming out of his office earlier. Her heart plummeted to her stomach as she grabbed Cassie's hand, then felt Lucas slip his smaller one into her other hand as he'd run back to her and his sister.

"Good afternoon, Beth," Matt greeted her as they came closer. He motioned to the dark-haired man beside him. "This is Jeb Winslow — Harland's brother. Jeb, this is Beth Morgan."

"Pleased to meet you, Miss Morgan." He tipped his hat to her and bent down to look at Cassie and Lucas. "I'm your uncle Jeb . . . your papa's brother."

Lucas scooted behind Beth and peeked out from behind her. Cassie held Beth's hand tight. Beth tried hard not to let the tension she felt show on her face, knowing that she had to take charge of the moment for the children's sake.

She tried to smile at Harland's brother. She could see the resemblance, but Jeb was younger, leaner . . . tougher looking. "How do you do, Mr. Winslow? I — we've been expecting you."

Jeb stood up straight and looked down into her eyes. Her heart leapt at the expression in them. He had the warmest brown eyes she'd ever seen. He smiled and nodded. "The deputy told me . . . you were engaged to my brother?"

"Yes." *Although, I wasn't sure. . . . But, no — now isn't the time to be thinking about any of that.* "Yes, I was."

He nodded. "It seems we've all suffered a loss. I appreciate your taking in the children."

"I wanted to. Actually, they were already living with me. The house at the ranch isn't fit for them yet."

"So the deputy said —"

"They are more than welcome to stay with me —"

"But I —"

"I have an idea," Matt interrupted. "Why don't you all come over to the café and have dinner with Emma and me this evening around six o'clock? It's beginning to get a little chilly out, and it might be easier to talk things over after a warm meal."

Jeb glanced at Beth. "If Miss Morgan agrees, that would be fine by me."

"Oh, can we?" Cassie asked. Beth knew Cassie loved eating at Emma's Café. Most of all, she seemed to enjoy the opportunity to hold Mandy, Emma and Matt's two-year-old.

Beth sighed with relief. It would be so much easier to talk at Emma's . . . with friends there. Her smile felt almost genuine this time. "Thank you, Matt. We'd be glad to accept your offer."

CHAPTER 2

As Jeb walked back to the sheriff's office with Deputy Johnson, he had a feeling that Miss Beth Morgan was not the least bit happy to see him. Oh, she had been polite and smiled at him, but it never quite reached her eyes. She sure was pretty, though, with those eyes the color of fresh honey and that thick blond hair pulled up onto the top of her head.

"Beth has taken real good care of Lucas and Cassie." Deputy Matt broke into his thoughts.

Jeb agreed. "I could tell that right off. But she won't have to, now that I'm here."

"We didn't know if you would come for them. Beth cares about them. She'd be glad to keep them if you —"

"Oh, I couldn't let her do that, Deputy. They are my responsibility, and they're all the kin I have left."

They reached the office, and Matt stopped

outside the door. He pointed to the café almost directly across the street with a sign that read EMMA'S CAFÉ. "That's my wife's restaurant. She serves the best food in town. I'll let her know you and Beth and the children will be having supper with us tonight."

"Thanks, Deputy. I appreciate the offer. I could tell Miss Morgan was a little uncomfortable talking to me. Maybe it will be easier over a meal, like you said."

"I hope so," Matt said. "We'll see you about six."

Jeb pulled his hat a little farther down on his head. "See you then. In the meantime, I have a few things I need to pick up at the mercantile, and I think I'll stop by the lawyer's office and make an appointment to see him tomorrow on my way there." He touched the brim of his Stetson and took off down the boardwalk.

Cassie and Lucas had all kinds of questions for Beth after Deputy Matt and Harland's brother had taken their leave. They continued as she helped them get ready to go to Emma's.

"How long do you think Uncle Jeb will stay, Miss Beth?" Lucas asked as she began to comb his hair.

"I don't know, Lucas." *But I hope it's not long.*

"Who was older, Papa or Uncle Jeb?" Cassie asked.

"I'm not sure, but I believe your papa was the oldest," Beth answered.

"Why does he limp, do you suppose?" Lucas's brow furrowed as he continued. "Do you think he might have been hurt in a stampede?"

"I don't know, dear. I'm sure that as a cowboy, he could be hurt in many kinds of ways." Beth tried to smooth down the cowlick in the young boy's hair, only to watch it immediately spring back up. She smiled and gave up. Turning him toward her, she straightened his collar and looked him over. "You look real fine, Lucas."

"Thank you, Miss Beth."

"How do I look, Miss Beth?" Cassie twirled around in her Sunday best.

"You look lovely, Cassie."

"Thank you." She turned to her brother. "We must be on our best behavior, Lucas. I would want Papa to be proud of us."

"I will, Cassie. Don't worry." Lucas slipped his hand into his sister's.

Beth turned to gather up their wraps, fighting back the tears that formed behind her eyes. He was being so brave. So was

Cassie. She could tell they were both nervous. So was she. She handed them their jackets and helped Lucas on with his. "Your papa would be very proud of you both . . . and so am I."

She pulled her shawl around her shoulders and tried to lighten the mood. "Let's head on over to Emma's. I wonder what her special is tonight."

"Oh, I hope it's chicken and dumplings," Cassie said, pulling on her own shawl. "I surely do love Miss Emma's dumplings. They're almost as good as yours, Miss Beth."

"Why, thank you, Cassie. That's a wonderful compliment, because I think Emma makes them best."

"I hope she has some apple pie, too. Do you think she will, Miss Beth?"

Relieved that their worries seemed eased for the moment, Beth chuckled. "I certainly hope so, Lucas. Liddy McAllister furnishes pies for her. Hopefully, she made a delivery today. Let's hurry and find out."

Even though it had turned a little cooler with the setting sun, the breeze had died down and the short walk to Main Street and Emma's Café was a comfortable one. The children's questions had ceased, and Beth wondered if their hearts pounded in their chests as fast as hers did at the prospect of meeting Jeb Winslow again.

Beth took a deep breath on entering the café. Jeb hadn't arrived yet, and she was a little relieved. It gave her time to compose herself. She certainly did not want him to see how uneasy she was about his arrival in town.

Emma came out of the kitchen just as Beth finished hanging Lucas's jacket on a hook by the door.

"Beth! It's so good to see you!" She gave Beth a hug and whispered, "I know this isn't easy for you. Matt told me that Jeb seems like a good man, though."

Beth only nodded. What could she say? It didn't matter if he was a good man or not; she didn't want him taking Lucas and Cassie away.

Emma patted Lucas on the head. "It's great to see you two also, Cassie and Lucas. Mandy has been asking about you ever since I told her she would get to see you tonight."

Cassie's face lit up in a bright smile. "Is she in the kitchen?"

Emma nodded. "She's upstairs with her papa. He'll be bringing her down any minute now. I've set one of the large round tables for us."

Just then Matt came through the kitchen

door holding Mandy in his arms. The toddler clapped her hands when she saw Cassie and Lucas. "Cazzie! Luc!"

The children hurried over to her, and she immediately held out her arms for Cassie to take her. The bell over the door jingled, and Beth and Emma glanced up to see Jeb entering. He smiled and immediately crossed the room to greet his niece and nephew.

Beth was pleased with the children's manners when they shyly greeted their uncle, but she was a little unsettled that they seemed so glad to see him again. She chastised herself. He was their uncle after all. Their father's brother. She should be ashamed of herself.

Matt welcomed Jeb and brought him over to introduce him to Emma. "Emma, this is Jeb Winslow, Harland's brother. Jeb, this is my wife and the owner of the best restaurant in Roswell."

Jeb tipped his hat. "How do you do, Mrs. Johnson? I have no doubt what your husband says is true. My mouth started watering a block away."

"Why, thank you, Mr. Winslow. That is the best compliment you could give me. I'd like to offer my condolences over the death of your brother. We didn't have a chance to get to know him very well, but from what we could tell and all that Beth has told us, we know he was a good man."

"He was that." Jeb nodded and turned to Beth. "And a good brother, too. He would have made you a good husband."

Beth forced herself to smile. "Yes, he would have." *I'm just not sure I would have made him a good wife.* She sighed. She certainly couldn't voice her thoughts. She motioned to the children instead. "He was an excellent father."

Emma motioned to the table she had set for them all. "Please, come sit down. I'll just go tell Ben and Hallie that we're ready to eat."

The children needed no coaxing to come to the table. Mandy was happy in her high chair, as long as she was seated between Lucas and Cassie. Beth sat down next to Lucas and held her breath until Jeb seated himself beside Cassie. She let out a small sigh and didn't know if it was one of relief or disappointment. For some reason, her heart had been pumping hard, as she wondered where he was going to sit.

"Hope you don't mind if your uncle sits by you, Cassie?" Jeb asked as he took his seat.

"I'd be glad for you to sit here, Uncle Jeb."

"You look a lot like your mother, Cassie. Mary was a beautiful woman."

The shy smile Cassie gave Jeb warmed Beth's heart.

"Did you know my mama well, Uncle Jeb?" Cassie asked. The wistfulness in her voice plucked at Beth's heartstrings. Harland's wife had only been gone a couple of years. Now the children had to come to grips with both parents being gone.

"I did. Mary was a wonderful woman. And she loved you and Lucas with all her heart."

Jeb's stature went up a notch as she saw the joyful expressions on the children's faces. At least he was sensitive enough to recognize that they needed to be assured of how much their parents had loved them.

Emma came back to the table and took a seat beside her husband. "Hallie will be right out with our meal. It is somewhat slow tonight, but I'm glad. I hope that I won't have to interrupt our meal to help out."

"It sure smells good in here, Mrs. Johnson. Smells kind of like chicken and dumplings."

Emma smiled at Cassie. "That's exactly what I made for us. I know it's one of your favorites."

"Is Mrs. Johnson right? Is that your favorite meal?"

Cassie nodded at her uncle.

"I'm kind of partial to it, too. But I don't think I've had that dish since the last time your mother made it for one of my visits. She was a real good cook."

Lucas propped his elbows on the table and rested his head in his hands as he gazed over at his uncle. "Did she make apple pies?"

Jeb grinned. "She sure did."

"Well, I'm sure I could never compete with your mother's cooking, Lucas, but Mrs. McAllister makes some of the best pies in town, and I just happen to have a fresh apple pie she made for our dessert."

"Thank you, Mrs. Johnson. I don't hardly remember what my mama's tasted like, but I know I sure like the ones you serve."

Beth grinned at the young boy. "He was hoping you would have apple pie, Emma. If I didn't know better, I'd think a little bird flew over and told you what they were wishing for tonight."

Hallie and Ben brought their food out, and after Matt said a prayer, the talk quieted down for a bit while they ate.

"Mrs. Johnson, I have to tell you, this has been one of the best meals I've eaten in a real long time. I would hate to have to be a judge between yours and Mary's dumplings, that's for sure. It would have to be a tie."

"Please, call me Emma. Thank you. I know that is praise, indeed — that I might cook as well as Cassie and Lucas's mother."

"Maybe that's why I like apple pie so good, do you think, Miss Beth? Because my mama made it?"

Beth smiled and patted Lucas's shoulder. "I think that might be it, Lucas. Now that you mention it, I'm quite sure it is."

"I think it's about time for that pie, too. Don't you, Lucas?" Emma asked.

"Oh yes, ma'am!"

Hallie was busy with several other tables, so Beth got up to help Emma clear the table and bring dessert plates and the pie back to their table.

Emma had warmed the pie up in the oven, and it came to the table smelling freshly baked. It was a hit with everyone, but it didn't settle too well on Beth's stomach. She knew that she and Jeb Winslow had to discuss the children. There was no way around it.

As if Emma read her mind, she suggested, "Cassie, how would you like to take Mandy and Lucas upstairs to our apartment and play awhile?"

Cassie grinned and bobbed her head. She looked at Beth. "May we, Miss Beth?"

"Yes, you may. For a little while."

Mandy clapped when Cassie lifted her from her high chair. "We go play, Cazzie?"

Cassie giggled. "Yes, we are going to play. Come on, Lucas."

Lucas took a last bite of pie and wiped his mouth with his napkin. "I'm coming."

Jeb chuckled, watching Lucas hurry to catch up with the girls. He seemed quite taken with his niece and nephew. Beth took a sip from the coffee cup Hallie had just refilled and tried to calm her nerves. She hoped no one at the table could tell how jittery she was about the conversation that was coming.

She saw Matt and Emma exchange a look before Emma stood up. "I know you two have things to discuss, so I'll clear the table and listen for the children. If you need more coffee or anything, just let Hallie or me know."

"I'll go up and check on the children." Matt pushed back from the table, taking a cue from his wife.

Jeb stood as the couple turned to leave the table. "Thank you both for getting me in touch with Miss Morgan and my niece and nephew. And Mrs. — I mean, Emma, thank you for the wonderful meal."

"You're very welcome. We'll be back down with the children in a little while. Take your time." Emma twirled around and headed toward the kitchen.

Jeb sat back down and took a drink of his coffee before giving Beth a smile. "It's *you* whom I need to thank most, Miss Mor—"

"Please, call me Beth."

Jeb inclined his head in agreement. "Only if you call me Jeb."

"All right, Jeb. You don't need to thank me. Really. I care about Cassie and Lucas."

"I can see that you do. And I do need to thank you." Jeb gazed down into his coffee cup before looking back at Beth. "I don't know what they would have done if it hadn't been for you taking them in."

"There are some good people in this town. Emma and Matt, or Liddy and Cal McAllister would have taken them. I'm just glad that they were with me." Beth closed her eyes and shuddered as she remembered the day she'd had to tell them that their father had died. She shook her head to clear the vision of the sorrow she'd seen in their eyes that day.

Jeb cleared his throat and nodded. "I'm glad, too. I really appreciate that they had you to turn to." He took a sip of coffee before continuing. "But now that I'm here, you can get on with your life and —"

"What are your plans for the children, Mr.

Winslow? Harland told me you liked to travel . . . go from job to job. That won't be easy to do with two children in tow."

"It's Jeb, remember?" He propped his forearms on the table and captured Beth's gaze with his own. "I realize that my life will be changing. I am ready to take on the responsibility."

Beth's pulse raced as his gaze never wavered. "Jeb, I will be more than glad to raise Cassie and Lucas as my own. They are comfortable with me —"

He shook his head. "I can't let you do that, Beth. They are my kin. I am the only living relative they have left, and I plan to take care of them. After I meet with the lawyer tomorrow and ride out to see the ranch, I will know better what to do. I would appreciate it, though, if they can stay with you for another night."

Beth's heart twisted in her chest at the thought it might be her last night with the children. *Dear Lord, please, if it be Your will, please let Jeb Winslow decide to let me keep the children.*

"Of course they can. They can stay with me as long as needed."

"Hopefully, we'll be able to get settled in a few days."

"Jeb, the house is still in horrible disrepair.

40

That's why the children were with me from the beginning. Harland felt it was important to get his herd started before he fixed up the house. He wasn't even living in it. He lived in a small room in the barn. He told me it was in better shape than the house, and he certainly didn't want Cassie and Lucas staying there like it is. They are more than welcome to stay with me until you can make the repairs that are needed." Beth held her breath and sent up a silent prayer as she waited for his answer. *Oh, please, Father. Let him agree to allow them to stay with me.*

Jeb took a sip of his coffee and stared into the cup for a moment before meeting Beth's gaze. He nodded. "Thank you for your generosity, Beth. I will take you up on your offer. It will probably be easier on them if they get to know me a little at a time before they come live with me, anyway. I'll go out tomorrow and try to get a handle on how long the repairs will take."

The relief Beth felt was immense. From all Harland had told her about Jeb, she figured he probably would not stick around long enough to make the repairs to the house. He had been roaming place to place for most of his life. She just hoped it wouldn't take long for him to decide to take off and leave Cassie and Lucas with her.

She prayed so. In the meantime, she would try to be pleasant and wait him out.

"I think it's a good idea for them to get used to you before you move them out to the ranch. You're welcome to come see them anytime, though."

"Thank you. I will be doing that for sure."

Matt and Emma came back into the dining room with the children just then, and Beth stood up. "I think it's time I got the children home. They have school tomorrow."

"I'll walk y'all home," Jeb offered, getting to his feet.

It was on the tip of her tongue to tell him he didn't need to, but Cassie and Lucas were his family, and it was his right to see that they got home safely. Beth and Jeb both thanked Emma and Matt for their hospitality amid the flurry of getting wraps and putting them on. She felt blessed to have such loyal friends. This evening would have been much harder on her if they hadn't been nearby.

Still in high spirits from an evening they enjoyed, the children alternately skipped, walked, and ran toward Beth's house. Jeb chuckled as he watched them, while he and Beth followed at a slower pace. But at the house, Jeb quickly told them good-bye and that he would see them the next day.

"You're welcome to stop by and tell us your plans tomorrow evening," Beth found herself saying as she gazed up into Jeb's warm eyes.

He smiled down at her. "Thank you. I will do that. I'll know more what needs to be done by then. You go on in and get warm. It's getting chilly out. And please tell the children I'll see them tomorrow evening."

"I will. Good night." Beth felt a little guilty for not asking him in as she peeked out the curtained window and watched him turn and pause a moment before stepping off the porch and heading toward the street. Still, she couldn't bring herself to utter the words.

The next day, Beth tried to keep her mind off of Harland's brother. It wasn't easy. Darcie was working the switchboard next to hers and had all kinds of questions once she found out he was in town and that Beth had met him the night before.

"Is he going to stay? What does he look like?" Darcie asked when there was a lull that afternoon.

"I don't know what he's going to do." Beth shrugged. "He looks a little like Harland." *Only he's much better looking and —*

"What do the children think of him?"

"They are happy to know they have family, I think. When they left for school this morning, they were looking forward to seeing him later today."

"You don't sound too happy about that, Beth. What do you think of him?"

"He seems to like the children, and he appears to want to take responsibility for them . . . but Darcie, what if they get attached to him and he decides to take off? Harland told me he never stayed in one place for long." Beth's switchboard lit up just then, and she gave her attention to her work for the next few minutes.

"Poor dears." Darcie shook her head.

Beth had no doubts that her friend was very sympathetic to Cassie and Lucas. Darcie's own father had passed away only a few years before.

"I can't imagine losing *both* parents in such a short amount of time," Darcie continued. "Maybe Mr. Winslow will settle down, knowing that they have no other living relatives."

Beth knew she should be hoping for just that, but she couldn't. She sighed. "I guess only time will tell. He did say the children could stay with me until he can fix up the house. That way they will have time to get to know him better."

"Maybe by then you won't feel so bad about giving them up."

"Maybe." But Beth was pretty sure she would never feel good about giving Harland's children up . . . to anyone.

That evening, Jeb showed up just as they were finishing supper. Cassie and Lucas were thrilled and quickly used the manners they'd been raised with to ask him if he would like a plate of the stew Beth had made.

"No, thank you. I ate at Emma's Café before I came over."

She supposed she should have issued an invitation for him to eat with them the night before, but the last thing she wanted was for the children to be any more eager to see him. She truly feared that they would get used to having him around just about the time he decided he would move on. She had to protect them the best she could.

Beth did offer him a cup of coffee and put a plate of cookies on the table for them all to enjoy.

"Thank you," Jeb said as she placed the cup in front of him and sat down across the table from him. "You know, I meant to ask about how you and Harland met."

"We got to know each other through correspondence."

"Oh?" His left eyebrow rose a little, and Beth could tell she'd probably given him more to question by her answer.

There was nothing to do but tell the truth. "I answered his advertisement for a mail-order bride."

"Oh." He took a sip from his cup.

She felt he was waiting for more information from her, but she wasn't about to tell him that she'd done it on a dare. That little bit of information wasn't any of his business. "We got to know each other through our letters, and after I accepted his proposal of marriage, he decided that he wanted to come out here and start a new life."

Jeb inclined his head and took another drink of his coffee. "I see."

No, I don't think you do. Beth didn't put her thoughts into words, and she was thoroughly relieved when Lucas changed the subject.

"Did you get to see the ranch today, Uncle Jeb?" Lucas then took a bite of the cookie he'd just grabbed from the plate.

"I did. Your father picked a nice spread, not too far out of town. It has a lot of promise. He left it to the two of you with me named as your guardian. I'm going to try to get it running the way your pa wanted it to be." Jeb took a sip of coffee and held it with both hands. He looked over the rim of the cup and into Beth's eyes. "You were right about the house. It is in real bad shape. It's going to take awhile to fix it up, what with having to take care of the herd."

Beth nodded in agreement. Her heart hoped that it would be too long for him to stay around. But that hoped dimmed at his next question.

"You mentioned the McAllisters last night. Do you know them well?"

"Liddy and Cal? Yes, they're good friends of mine. Cal was a lot of help to Harland."

Jeb leaned back in his chair. "Mr. Myers, Harland's lawyer, told me that they were taking care of the herd until I got here or the estate was settled one way or the other. I guess I'd better get out there and collect the cattle and pay them for taking care of them."

"I'm sure Cal won't expect payment. In fact, I'm confident that he would be glad to keep them for a while longer . . . until you decide if you're going to stay or not."

"Yes, well, we'll see. It was mighty nice of them to step in and help like that. I'll ride out to their place tomorrow. I need to do some more checking on the house. I do appreciate that you are willing to keep Cassie and Lucas until I can get it ready for them. Hopefully, it won't take more than a few months."

Beth's heart sank a little at the children's obvious excitement that their uncle seemed to want to make a home for them, and she immediately felt guilty for wishing they wouldn't like him quite so much.

"Can we come out sometime and help, Uncle Jeb?" Lucas asked.

"Why certainly. Maybe on some Saturday when you aren't in school." Jeb's gaze met Beth's from across the table. "As long as you finish any chores Miss Beth needs you to do. Is that all right with you, Beth?"

She forced herself to smile. What could she say? He was their uncle, after all. "That will be fine."

Jeb left Beth's house with mixed feelings. He sure was surprised that she'd answered his brother's advertisement for a wife. Surely she hadn't needed to do that. She was a lovely woman. What was wrong with the men in this town that she felt the need to become a mail-order bride? Jeb shook his head. Could they not see what a fine wife she would make?

Well, their loss would have been Harland's

gain. And Jeb had no doubts that his brother would have been a good husband to Beth. It appeared that they'd learned to care about each other through their correspondence.

She was probably still grieving, and he felt sorry for her. However, for some reason, Jeb had the feeling that she would like nothing more than for him to get on his horse and hightail it out of town and leave her and the children here. She seemed to have taken a disliking to him, and he wasn't sure why.

He almost wished he could say he felt the same about her. But he couldn't. He liked the fact that when he got to see the children, he also was able to see her. She was a good woman. That was obvious to him. She'd been taking wonderful care of Harland's children, and they adored her. He could understand why. She was pretty and sweet, and she truly cared about them . . . so much so that she would be happy if he would leave and let her raise them as hers.

But he wasn't going to do that, no matter how overwhelmed he felt at the prospect of raising them by himself. They were his kin — the only relatives he had left. And Harland had trusted him enough to want him to take care of Cassie and Lucas. Jeb was determined to raise them the best he could. With the Lord's help. And he needed all of His help he could get.

He strolled the few blocks to the hotel, sending up prayers and asking for just that.

CHAPTER 3

During the next few days, Jeb visited the children as often as he could while trying to settle his brother's estate. He made sure to show up well after he figured they'd finished with supper so Beth wouldn't mind if he offered a stick of candy each to Cassie and Lucas.

Small, but homey, Beth's cottage reminded him of the house in which he'd grown up. It consisted of a parlor, a dining room, and the kitchen downstairs, with the bedrooms — the children told him there were three — upstairs. There was a kind of warmth to it he felt the moment he walked inside that had nothing to do with the heat coming from the stove. He wondered if it was just because it'd been so long since he'd spent time in a house, but he didn't think so. More likely, it was because his brother's children were here, and it had been way too long since he'd been around family.

He tried not to outstay his welcome, but he loved being around his niece and nephew. They were full of stories about school and what happened there, and they were getting more and more excited about the upcoming fair.

"Beth is going to enter a couple of pies, and I'm going to help her make them," Cassie informed him one evening as they sat around the kitchen table while Beth was doing the dishes.

"Maybe I should teach you to make one and let you enter it," Beth proposed, smiling at the young girl's enthusiasm.

"I would love to do that!"

"I wish there was something I could enter," Lucas mumbled around the stick of candy in his mouth.

"Maybe we could enter some of your pa's livestock," Jeb suggested to the boy. "Cal is going to help me get the herd back over to the ranch tomorrow. I'll look them over again and see what he thinks."

"Oh, I would like to do that, Uncle Jeb!" Lucas grinned at him.

"Well, don't get your hopes up too high. But I will check into it."

Jeb glanced up just then to see Beth, a half smile on her lips, gazing at him from across the room. She looked away quickly, but not before he saw a faint pink color steal across her cheeks. It was the first time her smile seemed truly genuine. For the most part, she still seemed a little uncomfortable around him, and Jeb hoped that would change before too long. She tried to make him feel welcome, but he could sense that she wasn't at ease in his presence. He liked coming to her house and seeing the children, but he didn't like making her feel uneasy in her own home.

"Would you like the last of the coffee?" Beth asked, holding the pot up and shaking it slightly.

"No, thank you," he answered, even though he really would have liked another cup. "I'd better get going." The children had school the next day, and he didn't want to mess up their routine. He'd have to ask Beth exactly what that was before he moved them out to the ranch. That would be awhile yet. And he wasn't in too big a hurry. He rather liked seeing Beth along with the children.

It wasn't until after Cassie and Lucas were asleep that Beth finally allowed herself to contemplate the confusion she felt. Her pulse raced each time Jeb showed up at the door, but she sighed with relief each time he left for the night.

Oh, why did he have to come to Roswell and complicate things so? The children were already getting attached to him. How was she ever going to be able to protect them from an uncle who may or may not stay around?

Jeb did seem quite taken with them, however. Maybe Harland had been wrong about his brother. Just because he had moved around from one ranch to another for most of his life didn't mean he couldn't settle down, did it? If not, she sure hoped he realized it soon and moved on . . . for Cassie and Lucas's sake. They had suffered enough loss.

Besides, hard as she tried to get used to the idea that they would be moving out to the ranch, Beth riled against it. She wanted them to stay with her. And she owed it to Harland to make sure they received good care.

What could Jeb Winslow possibly know about caring for children? The only person he had ever taken care of was himself. The more Beth thought about it, the more frustrated she became. *Dear Lord, please help me with the resentment I feel that Harland's brother showed up. He is the children's uncle. I should be happy for them. Please, if he is going to have them, please help me to*

accept it and know that it is Your will. In Jesus'
name, amen.

Beth pulled her Bible close and opened it
for study, hoping to steer her thoughts away
from Jeb Winslow, for what truly bothered
her most right now was that she looked
forward to seeing Jeb almost as much as
Cassie and Lucas did. And that would not
do. No, that would not do at all.

There was a lot to do at the ranch, but Jeb
was pleased with the land his brother had
bought. It wasn't a big spread, but a family
could live on it comfortably. At some point,
one of the owners had planted apple trees,
and a nice orchard sat at the back of the
house. The trees were loaded with apples
that needed picking now. Next spring he
would get the children to help him plant a
garden outside the kitchen, and between
that and the livestock his brother had
bought, they'd be able to live well.

Now he stood at the edge of his brother's
pasture and gazed at the small herd of cattle
Cal McAllister had helped him bring over
from his place. Harland hadn't done half
bad in selecting the livestock to start his
ranch. And they sure hadn't suffered any
under Cal's care.

Jeb turned to the other man and held out

his hand. "I can't thank you enough for making sure this herd stayed together and in good health, McAllister. I wish you'd let me pay you for their keep."

Cal shook his head and Jeb's hand at the same time. "It was the least I could do. No one knew if you would be located or if you would come back here, and until things were settled for the children, it seemed the best plan."

"Well, I thank you. If there's anything I can ever do for you —"

"I'll remember your offer. In the meantime, if you need help getting the house in shape, just let me know. It's going to need a lot of work."

"Thanks. I appreciate the offer, but you have your own place to run, Cal. I'm hoping to have the house ready in a few months. Until then, I'll move into the room in the barn where Harland had been living. Beth was right. It is in a lot better shape than the house right now."

Cal agreed. "It is. One reason Harland got such a good price on this place was because the times had gotten bad for the people who owned it. The Nordstroms had planned on it being a real showplace, and they'd come out West with what they thought was plenty of money. But their plans were larger than their pocketbooks, and they ran low on cash before they could finish it completely. To try to finish it and keep the ranch going, they took out a loan with one of the banks in town and put their place up as collateral. The next year wasn't any better for them, and when they couldn't make the payment to his bank, Douglas Harper, the banker, had threatened to foreclose."

"He wouldn't give them an extension?" Jeb asked. Harper sure didn't sound like a banker with whom he wanted to do business.

Cal shook his head. "He wanted it for himself. There was no love lost between Harper and the people around Roswell, and rather than let Harper just have the ranch as he expected them to do, the Nordstroms put it up for sale. All they wanted was enough profit to get back home and pay Harper so that he couldn't have their land. Once Harland bought it, the owners paid Harper's bank off and moved back East."

"I think I'll steer clear of Harper's bank," Jeb said.

"You won't have to," Cal assured him. "Not long after Harland made the deal and the Nordstroms went back East, Douglas Harper ended up in prison for hiring someone to set fire to Emma's Café, trying to get her to leave town."

"He's still there?"

"Yep."

Jeb contemplated the house. The roof had a few old boards nailed over a spot or two that had obviously been burned. "How did it catch on fire?"

"Before Harland could get to Roswell, an electrical storm similar to the one that caused the stampede he died in sent a bolt of lightning through the roof of the house. This storm had rain in it, though, and it put the fire out fairly quickly but not before a lot of damage had been done. In the next few months, without anyone to care for it, the place deteriorated even more."

Jeb nodded. "Well, it can be repaired . . . and the land it's sitting on is prime. Barn is in real good shape. I'll be all right in there while I work on the house. Harland was staying in a small room in there. I guess he was going to use it to store tools and saddles and so on."

"Yep. That's what he planned. He worked on the barn first. The children were safe and dry in town with Beth, and he figured he needed the barn finished first to store winter feed for the cattle."

"She's offered to let them stay until I have the house ready."

"Beth is a good woman." Cal pushed his hat back on his forehead and looked him in the eye. "She would have made Harland a good wife."

"I don't doubt that for a moment. Have you known her long?"

"She's been here for about five years. She came out to help take care of her ailing aunt Gertrude. Beth liked it here, and after her aunt died and left the house to her, she decided to stay on. She's been working for the telephone company for the past few years."

"I can't help but wonder why she would have needed to answer my brother's advertisement for a bride, though. Are the men in this town blind?"

Cal chuckled and shook his head. "I don't have an answer for you, Winslow. Liddy and I have wondered the same thing . . . we surely have."

The only peace Beth had in the next few days was while she was at work . . . until word got around that Harland's brother had been found and was in town to take responsibility of the children.

Alma Burton was the first to mention it when her line lit up and Beth asked, "Number, please?"

"Beth? Is that you?" Alma asked.

"Yes, ma'am. What number do you need?"

"No number, dear. I just heard about Harland's brother getting to town and wanted to see what you think of him?"

Beth sighed. She wasn't supposed to carry on personal conversations while on duty, but there were no other lines lit up at the moment, and Mrs. Burton just seemed so lonely since her husband had passed away several months back. Beth just didn't have the heart to tell her that none of this was her business. "He seems nice enough, Mrs. Alma. But —"

"You want to keep the children with you, don't you, dear?"

"Well, I have come to care for them . . . but Harland didn't have time to make out a new will, and his brother was named as their guardian in the old one. I have no choice but to honor his wishes."

"Is Harland's brother married?"

"No, ma'am."

"Is he engaged to anyone?"

Beth caught her breath. She hadn't even considered the fact that he might be. "I don't know."

"Man needs a wife to raise children."

Beth hadn't even had a chance to get used to Jeb having the children. That he might marry and another woman would take her place in their affections didn't sit well with her. Several lines on the switchboard lit up just then. "Mrs. Alma, I have to go. The switchboard is lighting up."

"I'll talk to you later, dear," Alma responded before her light went out.

Beth breathed a quick sigh of relief as she connected the next few callers. The last person she wanted to talk about was Jeb. But her relief was short lived, because the next caller was Emma.

"Hi, Beth. Get me Matt, will you? But first, how are things going with you and Jeb?"

"All right, I guess. The children look forward to his visits."

"That's good, isn't it? He seems real nice. He's been taking some of his meals here, and Matt says he thinks he'll stick it out and make a home here for Cassie and Lucas."

Beth was sure Emma was only trying to assure her that the children would remain close by, but it didn't really help at the moment. It especially didn't help that her friends seemed to be welcoming Jeb Winslow with open arms.

"I guess time will tell" was all she said to Emma. "I'll get Matt for you."

She quickly connected the two lines and sighed. By the time she left for the day, at least six more people had asked about Jeb and if she thought he would stay. Seemed there was no longer any place she could avoid thinking of him . . . or talking about him.

Or seeing him. And she couldn't keep her pulse from racing at finding Jeb waiting outside the telephone office when her shift ended and she started home. Her heartbeat fluttered against her chest as he tipped his hat and smiled at her.

"Afternoon, Beth."

"Jeb, is something wrong?" He never showed up this time of day. "The children are still at school . . . they —"

"They're fine, Beth. I just had to come in for some supplies and thought I'd let you know I won't be coming back in tonight. I wanted to see if it would be all right for the children to come out to the ranch tomorrow, since it is Saturday. After they do their chores, of course."

Lucas had been hoping Jeb would take them out there, and so had Cassie. She couldn't say no. "Of course they may. I don't have that many chores they have to do. What time would you like me to bring them out?"

"Oh, I'll come fetch them. You are more than welcome to come, too. A woman's opinion on some of the things that need to be done to the house would be appreciated. Maybe we could have a picnic. The days are still warm."

She knew the children would love it. It sounded wonderful to her . . . even sharing it with Jeb. Or was it especially because of Jeb being there? She told herself it was because, if she went, she wouldn't spend the whole day wondering what Cassie and Lucas were doing and if they were having a good time with their uncle. And this way, she could see how Jeb took to having them around more than a couple of hours at a time.

"They would love it, Jeb. I could fry some chicken and make a cake."

"That would be nice. But I didn't mean that you would have to cook. I could pick up something from Emma's Café."

"No, that's all right. The children will be happy to help me make the cake tonight. And they'll hurry to do their chores, knowing there's a treat in store."

They'd been walking toward Beth's house all the while they were talking, and she turned to him as they reached her stoop. "What time would you like us to be ready?"

"I'll come get you about ten, will that be all right?"

"That will be fine."

Jeb pulled his Stetson a little lower on his forehead and touched the wide brim before turning to go. "See you all tomorrow then."

"See you then."

Lucas and Cassie's disappointment that they wouldn't be seeing their uncle that night had quickly changed to anticipation when Beth told them they'd be going out to the ranch the next day. They had talked excitedly about it while she made the cake and iced it for the picnic.

The children did hurry through their chores the next morning. Beth had fried the chicken while Lucas swept the floor and Cassie dusted. She'd made some escalloped potatoes according to the receipt in the *Fannie Farmer Cookbook* her mother had sent her for Christmas from back East this past year. It had only come out a few years before, and she'd been thrilled to get it.

She'd put some bread rolls out to rise and popped them into the oven right after she took the potatoes out. Everything would be ready just about the time Jeb came to pick them up.

When his knock came at the door half an

hour later, she sent Lucas to open it for him and hurriedly tried to brush up the strands of hair that had escaped from the psyche knot she'd worked hard to get just right.

When Jeb entered the kitchen, she'd just finished loading the potato dish and rolls into a basket and was covering it with dish towels to keep everything warm.

"Mmm, it smells good in here."

"Thank you, Jeb. Everything is ready to load into the wagon, I believe. This basket has the food in it and might be warm." She handed it to him and picked up the other one. "This one has plates, napkins, and cutlery. Lucas, you can carry it. Cassie, will you get the cake, please?"

Beth took off her apron and grabbed her and the children's wraps from the hooks beside the back door before hurrying outside. Jeb was instructing Lucas on how to put the food on the floor of the wagon, and Cassie was already sitting on the end of the wagon.

Jeb came around and helped Beth up onto the seat. She felt a little breathless as she sat down and he came around to take his seat beside her. It was a beautiful day, and she tried to concentrate on the clear blue of the sky, the birds flying south, and the traffic on Main Street as they made their way out of town. With wagons, stagecoaches, and single horses moving up and down the street, there was plenty to look at, but none of it could fully take her attention away from the man at her side.

Cassie and Lucas were asking a myriad of questions, and Jeb patiently answered as many as he could. The ranch wasn't far out of town. In fact, it was closer than Cal and Liddy's place. It was a lovely piece of land, east of town, near the Hondo River, with cottonwood trees and rich pastures. As they got their first glimpse of the house, Beth could only think what a shame it was that it was in such disrepair. It was going to take a lot of work to get it livable again — much less to turn it into the show home it started out to be. She shook her head. It certainly wasn't that now.

But the children didn't seem to mind as Jeb pulled the wagon close to the barn. They scampered out of the wagon and asked their uncle if they could look around.

"You can check out the barn while we set up the picnic, but wait until Beth and I are with you to check out the house. I haven't even inspected it all. But I know there are a lot of loose boards, and I don't want you to get hurt."

While Beth spread out the quilt she'd

thought to bring and Jeb brought the food basket over, they could hear excited chatter and laughter as Cassie and Lucas explored the barn.

"I suppose you are staying out in the barn?" Beth asked as she laid out napkins and cutlery.

"Yes. As you mentioned before, Harland had been staying there. There's a small room with a makeshift bed in it and a small stove. It's fine for now. I've certainly slept in worse places."

"Harland told me that you liked moving from one place to another."

"I've seen a lot of country." Jeb stared off in the distance before turning back to her. "But my wandering days are over. It's time I settled down." He grinned as Cassie and Lucas came running out of the barn. "More than time."

It was a perfect day for a picnic. The crisp, fresh air gave everyone an appetite, and by the time they'd finished eating, there was only half of the cake left for a midafternoon snack. Everyone pitched in and helped to put things up before they took off to look at the house.

It was of Queen Anne style, a two-story with the irregular roof pattern typical of the style, a corner tower, and wraparound porch. They mostly strolled around the outside of it, although Jeb did let them peek inside. But it was hard for the children to see past the ruin to what it could be.

On the other hand, Beth could picture it all refurbished . . . the parlor with gleaming wood floors and the fireplace at the center glowing with warmth. They went around the back, and she could see that it also had a back parlor. She caught a glimpse of a kitchen almost twice the size of her own.

"Oh my, it's big enough for one of the newest Sunshine ranges and a larger work-table in the center." She'd seen the new ranges in the Sears, Roebuck, and Company catalog and had thought to tell Harland about them when he got around to working on the house. They rounded the corner and found another fireplace on a side wall with windows on each side. "Oh, he didn't tell me it had a dining room, too! How lovely it would be with a sideboard and table and chairs."

Beth only now realized just how little Harland had told her about the house other than it needed work. She had no idea how big it was.

"How many rooms are upstairs, Uncle Jeb?" Cassie asked.

"There are three big bedrooms and a

small one up there. I'd let you go look, but like I said, there are loose boards everywhere and I'm afraid you might fall through. It can be a nice house. I can see that now. Thank you for coming out, Beth. Had you seen the house before?"

She shook her head. "No. Harland was so busy with the herd and all. . . ."

"Well, I'm glad you came out today." He turned to the children. "Come on. Let's get another piece of that cake, and I'll show you your papa's herd."

Cassie and Lucas needed no prodding. The house was interesting, but since they couldn't explore, they were ready to find another adventure. Picking apples was the highlight of the day, and Beth knew she'd soon be busy baking pies and making apple butter and still have apples to send in the children's lunches.

By the time Jeb took them back to Beth's, they were tuckered out. But they were happy, and Beth was glad to see the smiles on their faces as she sent them to wash up while she warmed some stew from the day before.

She surprised herself by asking "Would you like to take supper with us, Jeb?"

"Are you sure you have enough?"

"I do." She always had plenty. She should

have been asking him to eat with them instead of him spending money at Emma's or some other place in town. He didn't exactly have a place to prepare a meal at the ranch. And he shouldn't be having to spend all that money eating out when it was going to cost so much to get the house in working order.

"Thank you, then. I'd be happy to stay."

Jeb was glad he had stayed for supper. Beth was a wonderful cook, and sharing a meal with her and Cassie and Lucas served as the end of a near-perfect day as far as he was concerned. He couldn't remember the last time he'd had such a good one — only that it had been a very long time. Still, this was different. He was continually surprised at how content he felt when he was around the children and Beth, and he found that he didn't want the day to end.

As she told Cassie and Lucas it was time to get ready for bed, he knew it was time for him to go back to his barn. But that wouldn't be home forever. He had all kinds of ideas about the house after today and seeing Beth's enthusiasm about it. The children took their plates to the sink, and Jeb was quite touched when Cassie came around the table and gave him a hug.

"Good night, Uncle Jeb. Thank you for taking us to the ranch."

"Yes, thank you!" Lucas chimed in. "I really like it out there. I'd like to sleep in the barn sometime."

Jeb chuckled. "Maybe one day you can. But I think you'll like staying in the house a lot better once I get it fixed up."

"Could I maybe help you?" Lucas sidled up to Jeb and leaned against him.

"Maybe. Once I get those loose floorboards fixed."

"Thanks, Uncle Jeb."

Jeb patted him on the back. "You're welcome."

"Come on, Lucas," Cassie said. "Good night, Uncle Jeb and Miss Beth."

"Good night," Jeb and Beth responded at the same time.

Jeb watched as his niece and nephew went upstairs, then turned to Beth, who was refilling his cup. "Thank you for supper . . . and for the picnic today." He grinned and added, "And for leaving the last of the cake for me."

"You're welcome. It was a nice day. The children really enjoyed it."

"It was a great day. I have an idea what to do with the house now."

"What to do with it?"

Jeb nodded. "It needs a lot of work, and I didn't really know where to start. It took you coming out today to make me see the possibilities of it."

"It's going to take a lot of work . . . and money to repair it. It may not be worth it."

Jeb was silent for a moment.

Beth continued. "Jeb, Harland told me you liked the life you live. The going from one place to another. My house isn't very big, but it's big enough for me and the children. As I told you before, they are more than welcome to stay with me. You could come visit —"

"I realize I don't know much about raising children, Beth. But they are my family. They're my responsibility, and I want to make the ranch a home for them."

"But they need a woman's influence in their lives, too."

"I know they do." He took a sip of coffee before looking into Beth's eyes. "You could marry me, and they would have us both."

Had he just asked her to marry him? Jeb's heartbeat pounded like thunder in his ears. He could see the shock in Beth's eyes. It appeared that he had. He took a deep breath and waited for her answer.

She found her voice. "I — you can't mean that. I . . . you . . . that is a crazy idea." She plucked his cup out of his hand and took it to the sink. Then she spun back around to stare at him, her hands on her hips. "I can't believe you are serious."

Jeb couldn't either, didn't have any idea how those words popped out of his mouth, and he thought maybe he should take them back. Still, it rankled him that Beth found the idea of marrying him *crazy.* "Well, it isn't any crazier than answering a mail-order bride advertisement in the mail! You were ready to marry my brother sight unseen. Why not me?"

CHAPTER 4

Beth stared across the table at Jeb, at a momentary loss for words. She'd had a feeling he didn't approve of her answering his brother's advertisement for a mail-order bride, and she was certain of it now. And why not Jeb? She could see how he might be a little confused.

How could she tell him? She had barely admitted it to herself. But in the days before Harland died, she'd begun to have second thoughts about marrying him. There was something lacking in their relationship, and Beth had come to the realization that she'd acted foolishly in answering the advertisement. While she'd come to care about him, she hadn't been sure she could ever come to really love him . . . not the way she felt she should, and she hadn't been sure she could marry him.

But she hadn't told him. She'd been waiting for the right time, and it had never come. And, now that he was gone, she was glad she hadn't had to say the words to him. But one thing she knew for certain. She would never agree to marry another man she didn't know.

Still, it would be the perfect answer for keeping the children with her, and something deep inside wished that what Jeb was proposing could become a reality. But it couldn't — no matter how many somersaults her heart did or how fast her pulse raced each time he came near. After all Harland had told her about Jeb, she just couldn't believe he could commit himself to her and the children. It was only a matter of time until he took off . . . in spite of how good his intentions seemed to be.

Now, she tried hard not to let Jeb see how deeply his proposal had affected her. "Jeb, your brother and I corresponded for months before he moved out here. Enough to get to know each other a little." *But not well enough.* "You and I have only known each other a few days." *And you cause my heart to race in a way your brother never did.* "Besides, Harland told me you would never settle down . . . that you were used to going wherever you wanted to, whenever you wanted to. You aren't used to staying in one place."

"That doesn't mean I can't or won't."

Could he? Would he? Her heart thudded against her chest. If he did, might this be an answer to her prayers as a way to keep the children? Dare she allow herself to hope that he would stay? No. She couldn't. She would only be setting herself up for disappointment and heartache.

Beth just couldn't see him staying for long, and she had a feeling the only way she could deal with his proposal was to treat it lightly. "Well, I tell you what. If you stay around long enough to finish the house . . . maybe I'll just agree to marry you."

"Lady, I'm going to accept your challenge. I'll have it finished by Christmas. And when I finish it, you are going to have a decision to make."

Beth tried to ignore the warm wave of elation flowing through her at his words. She forced herself to laugh off his acceptance, praying he couldn't tell how flustered she felt. "By Christmas?"

"Yes."

"We'll see." Christmas was over three months away. He'd probably be long gone by then.

"Yes, we will." Jeb grinned at her as he stood to go. He sauntered over to the back door and took his hat off the hook beside the door. "We sure enough will. Good night, Beth."

Beth shut the door behind him and locked it with trembling fingers. Leaning her forehead against the curtained window, she took a deep breath and tried to will her rapidly beating heart to slow down. Had she really said she *might* marry him if he finished the house by Christmas? She thought back over the conversation. It appeared she had. And he had accepted her challenge.

She shook her head and pushed away from the door, trying to put it all out of her mind as she busied herself cleaning up the kitchen. But she couldn't get Jeb Winslow out of her mind. Part of her was sure he hadn't meant what he'd said . . . and another part was afraid to hope that he did.

Jeb made his way back to the ranch, but his mind was not on the road in front of him. It was back in Roswell, at Beth's. Just the thought of having her for a wife to help him raise Cassie and Lucas had his heart beating nearly out of his chest. He still couldn't believe he'd asked her to marry him . . . but now that he had, he wondered why he hadn't thought of it before now. After all, she'd agreed to marry his brother sight unseen. She loved Cassie and Lucas; that was clear. If she'd been willing to marry Harland, surely he could convince her to marry him.

Beth thought he wouldn't stay, but he was going to prove her wrong. Oh, he'd thought about putting the ranch up for sale and taking the kids back to Colorado with him. But that was before he'd thought the whole thing through and he'd seen the land Harland had left them. Roswell had become home to Cassie and Lucas, and they'd had enough to adjust to without having to move to a new town, knowing no one but him.

The ranch was prime land that would provide them with an inheritance from their father. And staying here, making a home for them on the ranch, might be his only chance to put roots down in a town he was coming to like a lot. That Beth might be part of all that . . . well . . . that was just the icing on the cake as far as he was concerned. Of course, he was going to have a job convincing her of that.

After taking care of the horses and settling down for the night, Jeb found the writing paper he'd bought in town earlier and sat down to write his boss. John Biglow was a good man, and he'd told Jeb to take what time he needed to get everything settled, but Jeb felt he owed it to John to let him know he wouldn't be coming back. He'd mail it on Monday when he went in to see the children. He needed to go to the bank and have his funds transferred from the bank in Colorado.

Tomorrow he was going to make a list of what he needed to get started on the house. It had suddenly become very important to him to get it ready for the children as soon as possible. Very important. Because he was going to prove Beth wrong . . . and he was going to try to win her heart in the process. He wasn't sure how to go about courting a woman, but he was going to do the best he could to do it right.

All day Sunday, Beth looked for Jeb to show up. Having Cassie and Lucas ask about him off and on all day hadn't helped. She'd watched for him at church and had been both relieved and disappointed that he hadn't shown up — relieved that she didn't have to pretend that his proposal hadn't had an effect on her and disappointment that he didn't appear to be a Christian.

It did feel good to be there, though, especially with all the confusion going on in her life. Minister Turley had a good message about waiting on the Lord, and Beth acknowledged that she needed to trust the Lord to help her sort it all out . . . in His time.

The children wanted to ride out to the ranch and check on their uncle, but Beth managed to get out of that by telling them that he was probably busy or he would have been in church.

"But what if something happened to him?" The fear in Lucas's voice was hard to ignore.

"I'm sure he's all right, Lucas. Besides, Cal and Liddy go right by there . . . I'm sure they will check in on him." She hoped. *Dear Lord, please let Jeb be fine. I don't think the children could take losing another family member.*

Beth searched her mind for something to do to get their thoughts . . . and hers . . . off their uncle Jeb. "You know, we could try our hand at making those apple pies we want to enter in the fair. Practicing sure won't hurt any, and we have plenty of apples since we picked so many at the ranch yesterday."

"Oh, yes! Let's do that," Cassie agreed.

The rest of the afternoon was spent peeling apples and making piecrusts. Beth used a combination of her aunt's recipe and one from the cookbook her mother had sent.

She let the children mix the apples, sugar, nutmeg, and salt together. Miss Farmer's cookbook called for lemon juice, too, but Beth didn't have any, and her aunt had never used it in her pies, so they didn't worry much about it. She did add just a scant teaspoon of flour to thicken the juices, just as Aunt Gertrude had.

She set the mixture aside while she showed Cassie how to cut the lard into a flour and salt mixture. Then they slowly added enough water until the dough formed a ball of sorts. Beth divided it into four separate balls and let each child take turns rolling out two of the balls of pastry dough into nice big circles.

They each put their circle into a pie dish, and Beth helped them add some of the apple mixture to each. She let them dot the apples with butter while she rolled out the remaining dough balls.

One pie was covered completely with the dough, but she cut the other piece of dough into strips and let Cassie and Lucas make a lattice pattern on the top of the other. Lucas thought it was great fun.

She showed them how to seal the edges and quickly slid the pies into the oven. "Now we wait until the kitchen is filled with the smell of baked apples and the crusts are golden brown. I think we may have some winners here. The fair is in a few weeks . . . so we can have a couple more practice sessions before then."

Beth didn't even have to ask Cassie or Lucas to help clean up. They pitched right in. Cassie wiped down the table and washed the utensils they'd used, while Beth started a stew from the leftover meat and vegetables they'd had for Sunday dinner. She'd made enough for Jeb, just in case he came into town. But he didn't. Maybe if she'd asked him before he left last night . . .

She put the pot on the back of the stove and adjusted the heat.

"Mmm, those pies are beginning to smell delicious." Beth opened the oven door to check on them and sniffed deeply as she got a warm whiff of the baking apples and cinnamon.

Too bad Jeb isn't here to smell these, Beth thought. Maybe she could —

"Can we give Uncle Jeb one of the pies to take home when he comes back into town?" Lucas asked as he swept the flour up under the table. "He sure don't have much food out there."

So much for keeping Jeb out of their thoughts. Beth chuckled. She'd been thinking the same thing. "I imagine we can."

She was pleased that the children had been observant enough to know Jeb's living arrangements weren't nearly as comfortable as theirs were.

"It will be good when he can get the house fixed up so he can stay in it instead of the barn," Cassie commented.

"I'd like to stay in the barn. Do you think I might be able to one day, Miss Beth?" Lucas asked.

"We'll see." Beth could fight it all she wanted, but Cassie and Lucas already cared a great deal for their uncle Jeb. All she could do was hope and pray that if he was going to up and leave them, it would be sooner rather than later. But what if he took them with him? What would she do then?

Suddenly tired, she poured herself a cup of coffee and sat down at the table. *Dear Lord, please help me to accept Your will in all of this.*

After Beth's reaction to his proposal on Saturday night, Jeb decided he'd give her a day to calm down. He certainly didn't want to get her more riled up. Although she'd told him if he stayed, she might consider marrying him, he was pretty sure that she hadn't really meant it. He chuckled, thinking back on the look of surprise that had come over her face when he accepted her challenge anyway.

Sunday morning, he saddled his horse and went to check on the herd. He'd been a lot of places, seen some nice spreads, but this piece of land his brother had bought sight unseen was one of the prettiest he'd ever laid eyes on. Oh, the house was in bad shape, but it could be repaired. And it would be a real showplace when it was. The land alone was worth much more than Harland paid for it. Evidently, he had just been looking for land at just the right time, and the Lord had been looking out for him. If Jeb ever had to sell the property for the children, they'd be able to get much more than their papa paid for it.

For now, he just wanted to make it a home for them. No matter what Harland had thought about his ability to stay in one place, he'd trusted Jeb enough to make him guardian of his children, and Jeb planned to see that his brother's trust wasn't misplaced.

That afternoon, he began making a list of materials he was going to need. He started taking up the rotted and damaged floorboards and was pleasantly surprised to find that there weren't quite as many as he'd first thought. But there were problems with the roof. Leaks were abundant and the main cause of the rotted boards. He needed to patch the roof as soon as possible, but that would have to wait until he could get the supplies from town. The fireplaces were in decent shape, but they needed cleaning. The staircase would need to be almost completely redone, too.

By the time Monday rolled around, he was thankful that Harland had left enough money to run the ranch and to make a start on repairing the house. But it wouldn't be enough to fix it up the way Jeb pictured it after hearing Beth's ideas. He sure was glad he'd set aside a nest egg through the years . . . and he could think of nothing he'd rather spend it on than making a home for Cassie and Lucas.

First off, he mailed the letter he'd written to his boss. Then he went to the Bank of Roswell and made arrangements to have his money transferred from his bank in Colorado. There were several banks in town — not counting the closed Harper Bank — but Cal had recommended this bank to him.

After his banking business was completed, he went to see about getting the lumber and the rest of the supplies he was going to need from the Jaffa-Prager Company. The huge mercantile sold just about everything on his list, and what they didn't have, they would order for him or he could order from the Sears and Roebuck catalog. He loaded his wagon with what he could and made arrangements for everything else he'd bought to be delivered to the ranch the next day.

He made a run out to the ranch and unloaded lumber, nails, and roofing material into the barn, glad that it, at least, was in good shape and he didn't have to worry about leaks. He checked on the herd, then came back to the house to take up more floorboards. He planned to go back into town when he knew the children were out of school and Beth would be home.

He was eager to see Cassie and Lucas. It surprised him how much he'd missed seeing them the day before. They'd quickly found a place in his heart, and he was determined to do the best he could to take care of them. All those years he'd been going from one place to another, he hadn't truly realized how much his family meant to him . . . until the only family he had left were his brother's children.

Now, as he worked in the house that would have been home to his brother, the joy he found in being around family again had a bittersweet quality to it. Jeb had taken off after both their parents had died, wanting to see the West, but his brother had tried to talk him out of it and had been trying to get him to move back to Arkansas for years. Jeb had stubbornly refused. Harland would have been so happy if Jeb had settled down nearby, but Jeb had no desire to do so. Until now — now that he realized how very much he'd missed in his absence.

Dear Lord, please forgive me for not being there for Harland when Mary died or not being nearby for Cassie and Lucas when Harland died. Please help me to raise them the best I can. I don't know much about raising children, but I know You will show me the way. And if it be Your will, please let me convince Beth that I will stay here and put the well-being of the children first. In Jesus' name I pray, amen.

With the Lord's help, he would raise the children the way Harland would want him to. And if it was the Lord's will, he'd have Beth at his side to help him.

On Monday, work was the only thing that kept Beth from stewing over Jeb and his proposal. She wondered if he would show up today. Cassie and Lucas had been wondering the same thing when they left for school. For their sake, Beth hoped he would. For hers . . . she hoped he'd already decided to go back to Colorado. If he stayed much longer, she was afraid she was going to begin to care far too much for him.

"How is everything going with Harland's brother, Beth?" Darcie asked during a quiet moment.

"The children are getting used to having him around. We went out to the ranch for a picnic on Saturday, and they love it out there. They had a wonderful time."

"What about you?"

"What do you mean?"

"Are you getting used to having him around?"

Beth shrugged and tried to evade the question. "I don't have much choice if he stays."

"He's awfully nice looking." Darcie grinned at Beth.

Beth sighed and shook her head at her friend.

"Well, he is," Darcie continued. "I had to go to Jaffa-Prager for Mama this morning, and he was there. It sounded like he was ordering all kinds of supplies to repair the house."

Beth's heart seemed to skip a couple of beats. It sounded like he planned to stay. She truly wasn't sure how she felt about it, but her heart seemed right glad. She ignored Darcie's first statement and tried to sound as if it didn't matter that much if Jeb left or stayed. "Oh?"

Darcie nodded. "Lumber, nails, all that kind of stuff."

Beth was sure Darcie knew what she was talking about. The younger woman just couldn't seem to help listening in on other people's conversations.

"Well, he's certainly got his work cut out for him, if he stays. The house is in pretty bad shape."

"It wasn't good when the Nordstroms lived out there."

"It sure has potential, though."

"Oh? You like it?"

Several lights lit up on the switchboard, saving Beth from answering right then. Yes, she liked it . . . and it would make a lovely home for Cassie and Lucas . . . but they had a good home with her, and the three of them were doing just fine. If Jeb left, they would be just fine. And she had to keep that thought first and foremost in her mind.

However, as she went up the walk to her house that afternoon and saw Jeb sitting on her porch, she had to admit that she wasn't being completely truthful with herself. The children would be heartbroken if he left . . . and she wasn't quite sure that her heart wouldn't break as well.

He stood and took his Stetson off as she approached. "Good afternoon, Beth. I hope it's all right that I came to see the children?"

"Of course. They watched for you all day yesterday."

He shrugged and grinned at her. "I thought maybe I outstayed my welcome Saturday night."

Beth's heart flipped against her ribs. Was he referring to her response about his proposal? She didn't know. She only knew that his very presence brought it all back to her. "Jeb, you are Cassie and Lucas's uncle," she said, struggling to keep her voice steady. "I wouldn't keep them from seeing you. Would you like to take supper with us? The children would be very happy if you would."

Jeb smiled down at her. "Thank you, yes. I'd like that. You're a good woman, Beth Morgan. My brother knew how to pick them, that's for sure."

Beth didn't know what to say. She felt she was living a lie by not telling Jeb that she'd decided she couldn't marry his brother, but she never got around to telling Harland, and she couldn't bring herself to tell Jeb now. She stayed silent.

"I have a few errands to run. When would be a good time for me to come back?"

"I'll be going to meet the children in

about an hour. We'll eat about six, but you can come before then so you can visit with Cassie and Lucas."

"I'll be here about five or so, then. Is it all right if I bring them some candy for later?"

"As long as you don't give it to them until after supper. Otherwise, Lucas won't eat anything."

"I promise." Jeb put his hat back on and tipped the brim. "I'll see you in a little while."

Beth watched him go, her hand at her chest trying to still the crazy beating of her heart. Oh, yes, she'd been lying to herself. She did care whether Jeb stayed or left.

She managed to get her pulse under control before Jeb returned. But only until he returned. There was something about his slow smile that made her heart skip a beat or two . . . or three.

Hard as Beth tried to keep Jeb from knowing that she was glad he was there, Cassie and Lucas left their uncle with no doubt as to how happy there were to see him. They talked nonstop from the time he arrived until Beth told them to tell their uncle good night and sent them to get ready for bed.

By the time Jeb stood to leave with the apple pie the children had saved for him, it was apparent that he'd won the affections of his niece and nephew. Cassie and Lucas loved him already.

As Beth shut the door behind him, it struck her that she had to be very careful to guard her heart with all her might . . . for she suddenly knew that she was in serious danger of losing it to Jeb Winslow. He already seemed to be stealing his way into it.

CHAPTER 5

In the next few weeks, Jeb seemed to split his time between working on the house and taking care of the herd during the day and visiting the children as often as he could, usually coming over in the early evening. But he'd also taken them on another picnic and more apple picking at the ranch, too. It didn't seem to matter what they did, Cassie and Lucas loved seeing him anytime.

Telling herself that it was only to give Cassie and Lucas more time with their uncle, Beth continued to ask Jeb to have supper with them. The children looked forward to his visits, and he even began to help them with their schoolwork while Beth cooked supper.

He still hadn't attended church, and Beth knew that was one reason she had to try to ignore the rapid beat of her heart each time he smiled at her or when their hands accidentally met handing a dish across the supper table. There was no way she could yoke herself to someone who didn't put the Lord first.

The much anticipated Southeastern New Mexico and Pecos Valley Fair was coming during the next week, and they were all looking forward to it. For the past few weeks, the *Roswell Record* had been full of planning details. Everyone seemed to be getting exhibits ready to be judged. Beth and Cassie had practiced their pie-making skills, much to Jeb and Lucas's appreciation. So far they hadn't tasted a pie they didn't love.

"Did you find a calf or horse to enter in the fair, Uncle Jeb?" Lucas asked on Tuesday evening as he finished his alphabet writing practice.

"I think we have a heifer that will show well. We'll enter her and see what happens." He shrugged and ruffled his nephew's hair. "Who knows? Maybe we'll place somewhere in the judging."

Lucas practically bounced in his chair at the prospect of winning a ribbon. "Oh, boy! I wonder what the McAllisters are going to enter?"

"Cal has a couple of calves he's entering. Next year we'll have more to choose from."

"Liddy is entering several pies and some

jelly and a few vegetables from her garden."

"Do you think we could plant a garden next year?" Cassie asked her uncle as she set the table.

"Sure we can. I don't know much about growing food, but we have some good soil and artesian water at the ranch . . . not to mention we're close to the Hondo River, too. I'm sure we can have a good garden. Cal says Liddy's is one of the best around, and they don't live far away."

Beth turned from the skillet of gravy she was stirring. "You know, you could enter the apples from your orchard this year. They are really good. I think our pies have a great chance of winning a ribbon, and it's your apples we'll be using."

"Oh, Miss Beth, that's a great idea!" Cassie said.

"It sure is," Jeb agreed. "They are sweet and crisp. And they surely do make a good pie."

"I can't wait until the fair!" Lucas could barely contain his excitement. "And I really want to see that alfalfa palace. Have you seen it, Uncle Jeb?"

As Beth began to bring dishes to the table, Jeb got up to help her. "I have seen the start of it. I rode out with Cal yesterday. He's taking some of his bales out and helping to put it up. I thought I might go over tomorrow and see if I can help."

"Ohh —"

No one could miss the longing in Lucas's voice. "Maybe we can take a ride out first thing tomorrow after school?" Jeb looked questioningly at Beth.

"I don't see why not." She took her seat at the table, and Jeb followed suit.

"May I go, too?" Cassie asked.

Beth nodded her approval as Jeb glanced at her once more. He didn't need her permission, but it was nice that he silently acknowledged that she was the one who'd been in charge of the children since Harland had died. "Of course."

Jeb waited for Beth to take a seat at the table before he sat back down. "I'll pick them up from school then, if that's all right."

"It will be fine." She waited for the children to settle down at the table, then asked, "Would you say the blessing, please?"

His prayers were usually short and to the point, and Beth wondered if he only said them because she asked and the children seemed to expect him to. They'd been used to Harland praying, and it probably never crossed their mind that their uncle wasn't as faithful a Christian as their papa had been.

"I wonder how tall they'll make that palace?" Lucas asked as soon as Jeb was finished praying. Obviously, his mind wasn't where it should have been any more than Beth's had been.

"I just can't imagine a palace made of alfalfa hay!" Cassie giggled.

"It should be something to see, that's for sure. I'd never even heard of an alfalfa palace until I moved out here. And with Aunt Gertrude not up to going . . . and working for others so they could, I've never been to the fair." Beth placed a fried chicken leg on Lucas's plate and passed the platter of chicken to Jeb.

"I hadn't thought a lot about it. I haven't lived many places where a fair like this was held. But it makes sense," Jeb commented, helping himself to the chicken. "With the hay harvested, tied into bales, and ready to store for the winter, it's handy to have it to put up shelter. It will protect the exhibits from possible rain, provide shade if it's hot and warmth if it turns cooler . . . and after it's over, it can still be used by the ranchers and farmers who've provided the bales."

"I have to admit, I am getting excited about it, too," Beth said. "We're going to make our pies on Friday evening."

Jeb slapped his forehead and appeared

distressed. "Oh, no! That means you won't be practicing your pie making anymore!"

Cassie laughed. "Don't worry, Uncle Jeb. We have lots of apples. We'll probably be making pies for a long time, won't we, Miss Beth?"

"Oh, I imagine we will." She couldn't help but grin at Jeb's show of relief.

"Whew." He ran a hand across his brow and grinned at the children. "I was worried there for a minute."

"We just don't have dessert for tonight," Cassie continued.

Jeb patted his shirt pocket. "Never fear. I stopped at the mercantile on the way over. I brought some gumdrops."

"I love gumdrops." Lucas grinned at Jeb.

"I know. But you have to clean your plate first," his uncle insisted.

"I will, Uncle Jeb!"

Beth exchanged a smile with Jeb at the young boy's exuberance. It was contagious.

The rest of the meal was spent talking about the fair . . . who they knew that might be entering some of the exhibits . . . what had happened during the day.

Beth thoroughly enjoyed mealtimes with Jeb and the children. It had become the highlight of her day. This evening, as she listened to them talk so easily to their uncle, one thing became totally apparent.

They adored him. And how could they not? He was really trying to build a relationship with them. At first they'd been a little hesitant to talk much around him. But as he asked more and more questions about them and how their days went, listening closely to what they had to say, they began to really open up to him.

Harland had loved his children, but he'd been a bit sterner with them than their uncle was. Now, they seemed to feel confident that they could talk to their uncle Jeb about nearly anything . . . and it was comforting to Beth that she wasn't the only one they felt they could come to. But would it last? Harland had said Jeb would never settle down in one place. But Beth found herself now praying that he would . . . for the sake of the children.

The next afternoon, as Jeb left the fairgrounds and started into town to pick up Cassie and Lucas to take them to see the alfalfa palace, he couldn't help compare the anticipation of seeing them again with the loneliness he'd felt leaving Beth's the night before. Of late, he always felt that way going back to the ranch. He would be glad to have the house ready so that he and the children could move in.

He began his mornings looking forward to riding into town to see them later in the day. And he really enjoyed suppertime with them. It'd been a very long time since he'd sat around a kitchen table and felt part of a family. And he was part of one now. He was the head of a family that now only included himself and his brother's children. But he had a feeling they'd all be missing Beth's presence once he moved them out to the ranch. Someway, somehow, he had to convince her to marry him and become a permanent part of the family. He sent up a prayer asking the Lord to show him how to go about doing just that.

As he neared the schoolhouse, he couldn't help but wonder what the children would have to say about the alfalfa palace. He was sure they were going to love it. He'd been helping Cal and some of his neighbors for most of the afternoon, and it was really taking shape. He'd enjoyed feeling part of the community and was eager to see it finished.

Cassie and Lucas were raring to go when he pulled up in his wagon, and they clambered aboard almost before he could come to a stop. He had to chuckle at his nephew as he climbed into the wagon.

"I thought the day would never end," Lucas announced, taking a seat beside Jeb.

"He's been really excited, Uncle Jeb," Cassie said sitting down beside her brother.

"You have, too!" Lucas told his sister.

"It is exciting," Cassie admitted. "How big is the palace now, Uncle Jeb?"

"It's big . . . and getting bigger every hour," Jeb answered, thinking about what it would look like to Lucas. "Just wait."

Jeb grinned at his niece and nephew's exuberance as he turned the wagon around and headed for the fairgrounds. It was northwest of downtown, near the Spring River, on the opposite end of town from their ranch. As expected, Cassie and Lucas were very impressed by the castle of hay. Although he realized it was quite large, Jeb hadn't really appreciated it quite so much until he saw it from their eyes.

Now, as Lucas craned his neck and stared up at it, Jeb chuckled. At eighteen bales high, not counting the turrets, it did look majestic.

"That's the biggest thing I've ever seen," Lucas uttered with awe.

"Me, too," Cassie breathed. "Oh, I wish Miss Beth was here."

So did Jeb. "We'll tell her all about it tonight. In the meantime, let's go take a closer look. Sun will be going down before too long, and Beth will be looking for us."

He made sure to stay close to them as they explored the palace. The designer was actually one of the local building planners in town, Michael Snow. He was on the site this afternoon, and when Jeb was introduced to him, he asked if he might be willing to come out to the ranch and give him a little advice on some of the repairs he needed to make to the house.

Mr. Snow nodded. "I'd be glad to. I drew up the plans for that house, and every time I pass by, I think about what a shame it is that it never was properly finished."

Jeb had been thinking the same thing . . . especially since Beth had seemed to think it held so much potential. For the last week or so, about all he'd been able to get done was patching the roof until he could fix it proper and some minor repair work inside. There were several things he just wasn't sure how to go about repairing . . . some of the trim had been damaged.

Jeb couldn't believe Michael was the one who designed the house. He sure was glad he'd come out today. "Do you have a copy of the plans? I'd sure like to see them, if you do. And if you have the time, I'd like your advice on how best to restore it."

"Now's the time to do it. I'll come on out

tomorrow morning with the plans, and we'll look the place over."

Jeb shook the other man's hand. "Thank you, Michael. I look forward to hearing your ideas."

By the time they started back into town, he wasn't sure who was the most excited. The children over seeing the alfalfa palace up close or him . . . contemplating what might be done to the house to make it the home of Beth's dreams.

Beth had watched the clock beside the switchboard for most of the afternoon. Since Jeb was picking up the children and she didn't need to be home, she'd agreed to work an hour longer for Martha, one of the other operators, so that she could run some errands for her mother before the stores closed. Darcie had just left for home, and the other operator, Jessica, was busy with the second switchboard.

Beth couldn't help but be a little jittery, even though she knew Jeb would take good care of Cassie and Lucas. She'd been the one responsible for them ever since Harland's death, and it was very hard to let someone else take over even partial care for them.

Alma Burton's socket lit up, and Beth put

the line pin in the socket. "Number, please?"

"Beth? That you?"

"Yes, ma'am, Mrs. Alma. Who do you need to talk to?"

"Well, I thought Darcie would be there, and I wanted to ask her something," Alma answered.

"She went home a little while ago. I'm working a little late for one of the other girls today." Beth glimpsed at the clock once more. "But Darcie might be home by now. Do you want me to ring her house?"

"No, that's all right. She's probably helping her mother get supper on the table for those boarders. What about the children?" the older woman asked. "Where are they?"

"They went out to the fairgrounds with their uncle Jeb."

"I saw him the other day over to the mercantile. He's a right good-looking man."

Yes, he is. But she didn't say it out loud. She waited for Alma to continue, but she wasn't going to let Beth off the hook.

"Don't you think he's handsome, Beth?"

Beth sighed. "He's nice looking, Mrs. Alma."

"How do Cassie and Lucas take to him?"

"They think he's wonderful." She held her breath, waiting for Alma to ask her if she thought he was wonderful, too, but thankfully, she didn't.

"That's good. I'll try to get hold of Darcie later. I still want her opinion on a thing or two."

"Yes, ma'am. I'll tell her." Beth disconnected the line and breathed a sigh of relief . . . until it dawned on her that Alma was likely going to ask Darcie what *she* thought Beth thought about Jeb. So far, she'd been successful in avoiding telling her friend that she was beginning to care about the man. She only hoped she'd been successful in hiding just how attracted she was to him.

"Mrs. Burton trying to pry information out of you, Beth?" Jessica asked.

"Bless her heart, I guess she doesn't have much else to do," Beth commented as her switchboard lit up and kept her busy for the next few minutes.

But Jessica was waiting for a lull. "You know, Mrs. Alma isn't the only one in town who thinks you and Jeb should get married and make a home for those children."

"Jessica! Who else? Who has been talking . . ."

"Beth, we work in the telephone office. We talk to half the town every day."

"Well, we aren't supposed to be gossiping!"

"We don't control what some of our customers have to say when we ask, 'Number, please.' You know that."

She did know that. And Jessica wasn't one to gossip. "I know. I'm sorry. I just don't like having everyone talking about me and giving their opinion on what I should do."

Jessica nodded. "I understand. But I thought you ought to know."

Both switchboards lit up just then, and there was no more time to talk before Martha showed up to relieve her. Beth eased out of the chair in front of the switchboard, and the other woman slipped into it. Martha and Jessica would work until Jimmy Newland came in to work from eight o'clock in the evening until eight o'clock the next morning. Things slowed down quite a bit at night.

Since Beth had the children to take care of and was considered the head operator, she only had to work weekdays. Darcie, Martha, and Jessica's shifts changed each week, along with a couple of part-time operators. But it was considered unseemly for the women to work alone at night, and it was the young men who worked mostly nights and weekends.

"Thank you so much, Beth. I really appreciate you staying late for me today," Martha said once she was settled at the switchboard.

Beth took her shawl off the hook by the door. "You're welcome, Martha. The children were with their uncle so it wasn't a problem. But they should be showing up anytime now. I'd better get on home."

"I saw them coming into town on my way here. Harland's brother certainly is a nice-looking man."

Beth kept silent as she drew her shawl around her. To agree somehow seemed disloyal to Harland. He had been nice looking, but not near as handsome as Jeb. Or maybe it was that she wasn't as attracted to —

"Oh, I'm sorry, Beth. Of course, Harland was a good-looking man, too."

Beth smiled at the other woman, relieved that she'd broken into her thoughts. "Neither of the Winslow brothers had reason to cover their faces, that's for sure."

"You're right about that." Martha chuckled and waved as Beth opened the door and headed out of it.

"Good night, Martha. Good night, Jessica." Wondering if Jeb and the children would be at her house when she got there, Beth hurried home. She tried to think what she would fix for supper. There was some stew from the other night she could heat up. It would be good with a pan of corn bread.

Seeing Jeb's wagon outside her house set her heart to pounding, and she hurried her pace. She entered the kitchen to find him lighting a lamp and Cassie supervising Lucas as he pumped water into a jar from the kitchen sink.

"Miss Beth, were you at the telephone office?" Cassie asked. "We were thinking of ringing there to see. It felt strange that you weren't here when we came in."

"I worked a little late for one of the girls."

"Uncle Jeb told us that you would probably be tired and that we could all go to Emma's Café for supper," Lucas informed her.

Beth's gaze flew to Jeb. "Oh, that's not necessary —"

"After working late, I'm sure you don't feel up to making supper, Beth. Let me take us all to Emma's."

"No, it's all right. I have stew to heat up, and I can make some corn bread."

"Only if you let me treat on Friday or Saturday night, then. I eat here most nights, Beth. The least I can do is treat you to an evening free from cooking once in a while."

"Look, Miss Beth," Lucas said from

behind her.

She turned to find him holding the jar he'd filled with wildflowers in water. "Oh, Lucas, they're lovely."

"We saw them on the way home, and Uncle Jeb thought you might like some."

Beth took the jar of flowers from Lucas's small hands and turned to Jeb. "That was very nice of you."

He shrugged and grinned. "We all thought they were pretty and agreed that you might think so, too."

"I do. They are beautiful, and I do love flowers of any kind. Thank you all." That they thought of her while they were out pleased her immensely. That they had stopped and picked them just for her touched her deeply. That Jeb was the one who suggested it had her heart fluttering against her ribs. Beth turned and busied herself by putting the jar in the middle of the kitchen table, hoping that Jeb couldn't see just how much she was affected by his actions.

Good to his word, Michael Snow came out to the ranch the next day with the original house plans and gave Jeb some advice on how to go about making repairs. He knew Beth would love Michael's suggestions. But, even if things didn't end up like he wanted them to with her, he and the children would have a wonderful house to call home. Jeb could hardly wait to get started.

"I'm glad this house will have someone who cares about it living in it," Michael said. "It's not quite as bad as it appears from the outside. I don't think it will take all that long to get it in good shape."

"That's good to hear. I would like to have it finished by Christmas."

Michael nodded. "I think that's possible . . . if we are spared any really bad weather. Refurbishing it and making it the home it was meant to be will definitely raise the value of the land if you ever decide to sell out."

Selling out wasn't in Jeb's plans, but knowing that he was doing the best he could to enhance the land Harland had left to his children gave him a good feeling.

"I'll see you later at the fairgrounds?" Michael asked as he mounted his horse.

Jeb nodded. "I'll be there."

He strode toward the barn, now excited about the house and the suggestions and advice Michael had given him. Due to the Nordstroms' depleted funds, the house lacked many of the decorative elements — the trim and finishing work.

He tried to remember some of the things Beth had mentioned when she'd looked around. Oh, he knew he might never convince her to marry him, but he wasn't going to give up without trying. She'd liked the flowers he and the children had brought her. Jeb had caught her looking at the bouquet several times throughout supper last night. He had been surprised at how good it made him feel to know he'd done something that really pleased her.

Up until last night, when they'd come into an empty house, Jeb hadn't realized just how much Beth did for his niece and nephew. She worked outside the home all day and still managed to take wonderful care of Cassie and Lucas . . . giving them the extra attention they needed, keeping their clothes clean, and feeding them well — not to mention that she even fed him most of the time now. And all of this because she'd been going to marry his brother. Jeb hoped Harland had appreciated her and realized how the Lord had blessed him with such a good woman . . . two great women, counting Mary.

Jeb was just hoping and praying for one good woman. He was pretty sure he'd found her in Beth. And if it was the good Lord's will, she'd be moving into the ranch house with him and the children come Christmas.

Jeb saddled up his horse and turned toward town. He was looking forward to the start of the fair and taking Cassie and Lucas . . . and Beth.

CHAPTER 6

The fair started on Tuesday, and Beth couldn't quite tell who was more excited — the children or Jeb. It was all any of them had talked about for the past week. But actually, the fair had been the talk of the whole town. On the first day, Mayor Adams had welcomed the governor, who'd made the trip down from Santa Fe to give an opening address.

There was much talk — both in the town newspaper, the *Roswell Record,* and all along the telephone lines — about the goings-on. Working at the telephone office, Beth had a good idea of who had entered the exhibits and what they'd entered . . . even who they were hoping to win over.

Liddy McAllister was entering her apple and peach pies. Beth didn't expect to win over Liddy, but Cassie was excited about entering something in the fair, and Jeb and Lucas had told them that their pies were excellent.

Jeb had decided to enter some of his apples, and although he didn't think he'd win, he entered a two-year-old Hereford in the cattle category. He promised Lucas that they would enter more livestock the next year, when he'd know more what to enter after this fair.

According to Darcie, Alma and several of her friends were entering quilts they'd made, and Alma was hoping to win first place. Of course, Myrtle Bradshaw, Doc's wife, and Nelda Harrison were both hoping for the same thing.

School was dismissed early each day, and Jeb came into town to pick up Cassie and Lucas each afternoon to take them to the fair, but it would be Saturday before Beth could go. Each night at the supper table, they entertained her with stories about what was going on.

There were horse races every day, and one of Cal McAllister's horses, Rusty's Son, won the first two days.

Cassie told about the ladies' textile exhibits with all kinds of needlework entered, and the cooking and baking exhibits. The cakes, pies, jellies, and preserves would be judged on Saturday. Beth could hardly wait until then. Not so much for the judging, but because everyone was having such fun and she would finally be able to join them.

On Thursday night, Lucas burst into the kitchen, laughing. "Miss Beth, you'll never guess what happened today!"

She turned from the stove and couldn't help but grin at him. "What happened, Lucas?"

"Well, we thought there was a fire in the palace!"

Beth placed a hand over her suddenly pounding heart. "Oh, that doesn't sound very funny, Lucas. No one was hurt, were they?"

Lucas shook his head. "No. 'Cause there wasn't a fire." He began to laugh again.

Jeb and Cassie chuckled as Lucas tried, but couldn't get more out for his spurts of laughter.

"You tell about it, Uncle Jeb," Cassie suggested.

"Well, like Lucas said, there wasn't a fire. Come to find out, Councilman . . . ?" Jeb looked at the children with a question in his eyes.

"Bagley," Cassie reminded him.

"That's right. Councilman Bagley evidently lit up his pipe back in one of the exhibits, and with all that puffing, smoke was just a-billowing out around him. Someone yelled, 'Fire!' and I grabbed the children up and we rushed outside."

Jeb started chuckling then, and it took a moment for him to continue. "You should have seen the councilman's face when he came out of there with his wife a-yellin' at him, telling him what for with his pipe in her hand."

"Oh, dear." Beth put a hand to her mouth and began to chuckle.

"But that's not even as funny as what happened at the fair several years back," Cassie giggled. "Tell her Uncle Jeb."

"Well." He chuckled and paused a minute. "One of the old-timers told us about something that happened at the fair of 1893. And Cal said it really did happen. One of the bales of hay caught fire from a turned-over lantern, and even though they got it put out right away, everyone was rushed out of the palace. Most all of the people were outside when they turned to see one of the men carrying out a lady. Said they figured she just passed out from the smoke or something, but come to find out . . ." Jeb broke off and laughed as Cassie and Lucas burst into giggles again.

Beth waited. What could possibly be funny about a woman fainting or passing out?

Finally, having to know, she said, "Well, come to find out what?"

"It weren't a woman at all, Miss Beth," Lucas shouted, bursting into laughter again.

"It was a" — Cassie stifled a giggle to get it out — "it was a dress form, all dressed up in one of the dresses entered in the ladies' textile exhibit." She couldn't contain the laughter any longer.

"Oh, dear." Beth chuckled. "I wonder what he said when he saw it wasn't a woman?"

"It was a cowboy from Lincoln County, is what I heard." Jeb was trying hard not to laugh as he continued, "He said, 'Well, I sure 'nough thought she was the lightest woman I'd ever carried.' Then he tipped his hat to the form and to everyone watching and skedaddled out of there."

Beth's chortle quickly turned into laughter that had her doubling over, as she pictured the sight. Oh my, oh my. She couldn't wait until Saturday.

When Saturday finally rolled around, Beth was up early, frying chicken and making a picnic lunch. Most everyone took food to the fairgrounds, and Liddy McAllister had told Beth not to worry about sending food during the week, because she would have plenty for Jeb and the children. Liddy was such a good woman and friend. Beth wanted to reciprocate and had told Liddy that she would help provide the food for today.

She and Cassie had made their pies the night before, and they were ready to go for the exhibit. But those were for the judges, so they'd made an extra one for their own lunch.

It was a beautiful day, warm and sunny, as it often was at the beginning of October. Knowing it would be dusty at the fairgrounds, Beth chose a tan skirt and beige shirtwaist with a wide collar and front ruffle.

Even though Cassie and Lucas had gone to the fair every day, they seemed almost as excited as Beth felt. Of course, part of that was because they wanted her to see everything. When Jeb showed up with his wagon and helped her load the food into it, he seemed in high spirits, too.

The children scampered up into the wagon bed, and Jeb held Beth's elbow to assist her in getting up onto the wagon seat. He took his place beside her and smiled. "Ready?"

"Oh yes, I am."

Wagons, buggies, and surreys filled the outskirts of the fairground; and lots of men, women, and children were making their way to the famous alfalfa palace. It was impressive, Beth thought as they started toward it. It was comfortable inside, not too warm or too cool. And although dim at first, once inside, Beth found each exhibit had lanterns hung from wooden rafters that had been layered between the bales of alfalfa.

Cassie knew right where to go to enter their pies for judging. Although Beth had supervised her, the young girl had done all the work on these pies, and they were entered in her name. They were placed on a table along with about twenty others, and Beth and Cassie were told that the judging would be finished by noon.

"Guess what, guess what?" Lucas asked excitedly as he came running up to them. He and Jeb had checked out the entries for the fresh fruit.

"We got first place for our apples!"

"Why, that's wonderful news, Lucas! Let's go see!"

Jeb was grinning ear-to-ear. "I know I didn't plant those trees in the orchard, but it sure makes me happy that whoever did certainly knew what they were doing."

"Well, I'm hoping that blue ribbon carries over to our pies!" Beth exclaimed as they walked over to the fresh fruit and vegetable display. There, right beside the basket of apples and the sign that read WINSLOW RANCH APPLE ORCHARD, was a big, first-prize ribbon.

Cassie hugged her uncle. "Papa would be so happy! Wouldn't he, Miss Beth?"

Beth's gaze met Jeb's. It was the first time either of the children had mentioned their father in a while. She hoped it meant their sorrow was easing a bit. "He certainly would, Cassie."

They browsed through the other displays. There were fruits and vegetables of all kinds — corn, wheat, oats, alfalfa, pumpkins, squashes, beets, carrots, cabbages, turnips, and parsnips. There were also sweet potatoes, Irish potatoes, watermelons, onions, and peaches.

They ran into the McAllisters, who were inspecting all of the entries, too. Liddy's and Cal's daughters, Grace and Amy, had entered a couple of watermelons they'd planted and tended on their own, and they were thrilled at the first-place win. The McAllisters' boys — Matthew, who was three, and baby Marcus — were a little young to enter anything, but they seemed to be enjoying everyone else's excitement.

"Those sure look like good melons," Lucas said. Everyone there knew he was a big fan of watermelons.

"We brought a couple to have when we eat," Cal assured him.

"But that won't be for another hour or so," Jeb reminded his nephew.

"Well then, let's go see the animals," Lucas suggested, changing the subject and jumping up and down in excitement. "Maybe we have a ribbon for the Hereford you entered, Uncle Jeb!"

Jeb swung him up onto his shoulders as they headed for the livestock exhibits. "I don't think we better count on that this year. But maybe next."

Beth's heart skipped several beats at his words. Would he be here next year? He talked so confidently about staying, but all she could remember was Harland saying his brother would never settle down. Never.

By noon, they'd inspected all of the livestock exhibits. Jeb was right. His Hereford didn't win anything, but they congratulated Cal on his first-place win. They ran into Matt and Emma, who had left the café in the capable hands of Ben and Hallie for the afternoon. They had Mandy with them, and she appeared to be having a great time.

It was time to find out who won the baking exhibit, and they all hurried over to the women's exhibition wing of the palace. The judges were just finishing tallying their score, so Beth and Cassie and Liddy and her girls, Grace and Amy, all held hands and waited.

There was no major announcement, only ribbons placed in front of the entries. Once the judges finished, the ladies hurried up to the table. Cassie gave a discreet little squeal when she saw the second-place ribbon gracing her pie. Beth enveloped her in a hug, while she congratulated Liddy for taking first place.

"Thank you," Liddy said. "But I think I've got major competition in the coming years if Cassie came in second at her age!" She hugged the young girl when Beth let go. "Great job, Cassie!"

Lucas grinned up at his sister. "I just knew you were going to win, Cassie! Mama and Papa would be proud of you!"

Jeb hugged his niece, too. "I knew when I had a bite of that pie you made the other night that you were going to win a prize."

"I'm gettin' hungry just looking at these," Cal admitted.

"Me, too," Matt added.

"Well, I guess it's time we feed these men, if they're going to have strength enough for the races this afternoon," Liddy said.

As they made their way out to the grounds and to their wagons to gather the food and quilts they'd brought, Beth couldn't help but notice how many people said hello to Jeb. Of course, he'd helped with building the alfalfa palace, but he seemed to have gotten to know a lot of people in the area in a very short period of time. Beth supposed that if one moved around as much as Jeb did and never stayed anywhere very long, one had to make an effort to get to know people quickly.

After sharing the food Beth, Liddy, and Emma had brought, they went to watch the horse races and cheered along with Matt and Jeb as Rusty's Son, Cal's horse, came in first place again. Then they split up, with the men and boys going to the other horse races and the women and girls checking out the ladies' textile exhibits. There were all kinds of entries in quilting, fine sewing, crocheting, knitting, and embroidering.

Alma's quilt did win first place, with Myrtle's coming in second. Beth and the others moved through the many samples of ruffles, tucks, puffs, edging, lacing, fluting, and openwork done with thread. The women of eastern New Mexico were quite skilled in all areas.

At midafternoon, Beth, Liddy, Emma, and the girls met up with Jeb, Cal, Matt, and the boys at one of the food vendors for tall glasses of lemonade or tea. After that, they all took in the other races. First were the bicycle races, followed by the fifty- and one-hundred-yard foot races.

When Jeb and Lucas signed up for the three-legged race, Matt and Cal did, too. Then Beth and Cassie, along with Emma and Liddy and their girls, as the men began the race on all fours. Beth laughed until her side hurt as she watched Jeb and Lucas take a tumble and try to get up. They finally righted themselves about the time Matt and Cal took a fall directly in front of them.

Seeing the four of them try to right themselves and get back into the race had tears of laughter streaming down the faces of Beth and the rest of her entourage. Still, Jeb and Lucas managed to come in third, while Matt and Cal came in fifth.

As the day came to a close, Beth truly hated for it to end.

In the days following the fair, Jeb couldn't remember when he'd had such a wonderful time. It had felt so right to share the day with Beth and his niece and nephew. He became more determined than ever to get the house finished by Christmas. He wanted the children in their own home, and he prayed the good Lord would see fit to help him win Beth's heart so that she'd be with them all.

The plans Michael Snow gave him were just what Jeb needed to envision the house as it should be. He was sure the children and Beth would love the house when it was finished.

After talking about the fair for months, all the planning for it, and then the actual preparations for it, there seemed to be a little letdown in town for the next few weeks. The mood at Beth's house was no different. But it didn't last too long after Jeb brought the Sears and Roebuck catalog over one evening.

For the next week or so, their evenings revolved around poring over all the items offered in the large book . . . with Jeb paying close attention to the items that particularly caught Beth's eye.

There were several ranges, and Beth gave much attention to each one, but it was a huge range called the Sterling Sunshine steel plate range that really caught her eye. There was also a large worktable called the Handy kitchen table she kept going back to. According to the advertisement, it had two large flour bins and two drawers for utensils and so on.

There were bed sets and parlor sets, dining room tables and sideboards. That catalog gave Jeb more insight into Beth's likes and dislikes in a house than several months of asking probably would have. He pored over it back at the ranch, too, making note of any new thing that Beth or the children had pointed out that he might be able to afford for the house.

During supper at Beth's on a Friday night, several weeks after the fair, the children began to talk about the next month and Thanksgiving. The days were flying by, and Jeb couldn't believe how fast November was approaching.

"What do you do for Thanksgiving, Miss Beth?" Lucas asked. "We've been learning about the first settlers. The other children were talking about what all their families do, but I don't remember what we used to do . . . do you, Cassie?"

Jeb's heart twisted at the thought that Lucas couldn't remember what they did for Thanksgiving. Of course, he'd been young when his mother passed away —

"Mama used to roast a turkey or bake a big ham. We had all kinds of good things to eat. But last year . . ." Cassie shook her head. "I don't remember what we did, Lucas."

Beth quickly took Jeb's cup of coffee to

the stove to refill it, but not before he caught the gleam of a tear in her eyes. He'd had to bend his head and blink a couple of times himself to keep from giving his own emotions away to the children.

From across the room, Beth cleared her throat before speaking. "Well, my aunt and I always had a nice meal, and we usually spent the day with one of her friends. We'll plan for a wonderful day. We can have turkey or a ham — and, Cassie, you and I can pick out a few new pies to try our hand at. I've never made a pumpkin pie, but the pumpkins are really growing this year."

"Oh, I'd like that!" Cassie replied.

"Can we have apple pie, too?" Lucas asked.

Jeb had a feeling Lucas would always love apple pie. It seemed to be the only kind he could remember his mama making. His heart warmed when Beth answered his nephew.

"Of course, Lucas. I can't imagine having Thanksgiving without it." She set the fresh cup of coffee in front of Jeb.

"Thank you, Beth." He hoped she knew his gratitude was for more than the coffee. She was wonderful to his brother's children. No one could doubt that she cared deeply for them. And there was no denying that he'd come to care for *her* more each and every time he saw her. He thought about her first thing in the morning and last thing at night, and there was no denying the way his heart pounded in his chest when she welcomed him into her home of an evening.

"You're welcome. Anything special you'd like to have on the menu, Jeb?"

"Hmm . . . it's been a long time since I've had a big Thanksgiving dinner. Even longer since it's been with family. I seem to remember my mama" — he smiled at Lucas and Cassie, who gave him their undivided attention — "*your* grandmother, used to make some kind of pudding."

"Could it have been a rice pudding?" Beth asked, turning her head to the side as she thought.

He loved the way the lantern light shimmered on the golden strands of her hair. "Might have been."

"Or maybe a bread pudding?"

And the way her eyes sparkled in the light. "That could have been it."

"Did it have a sweet sauce served over it?"

"I think so." But he didn't know how it could be as sweet as her lips appeared to be in the lamplight. He was certain no sauce could be as sweet as a kiss from Beth might be. It suddenly occurred to him. He'd been thinking about doing that a lot lately — kissing Beth.

Beth nodded and smiled. "That sounds like a bread pudding. I'll see if I can find a receipt for it."

"That's not necessary. I'm thankful enough just to be taking dinner with family."

"Uncle Jeb?" Lucas stared at him from across the table, his chin propped in his hand.

"Yes, Lucas?"

"Why don't you go to church? You believe in God, don't you?"

There was silence at the table — as if everyone was waiting for his answer. "Why, of course I believe in God, Lucas. I can't imagine life without Him in it. Why, your papa and I were baptized in the Arkansas River on the very same day. I usually read my Bible every night and . . . on Sundays, I kind of get on my horse and ride and contemplate on what all the Lord has done for me . . . all kinds of things like that." Cassie and Lucas kept looking at him as if they expected more of an explanation. He could only tell the truth.

"I don't rightly know why I don't go to church. I've just never lived close enough to one to go every Sunday, and I guess I just didn't think about it now that I do." And now that he thought about it, Jeb wondered why it hadn't occurred to him to attend church with them.

"Well, will you come this Sunday?" Lucas asked right out.

"Yes, I will." Jeb glanced over at Beth and saw a half smile on her lips. She seemed pleased, and he wished he'd thought to accompany them on Sundays before now. He sure did wish that. "I will come to church on Sunday, I promise."

That seemed to be all that was needed. "Good," Lucas replied, grinning ear to ear.

Beth sat at the kitchen table long after Jeb left for the night and the children were fast asleep. Would he be at church on Sunday as he'd promised Lucas? So far, he'd kept his word to the children. But she was afraid to hope that he'd show up . . . she'd been praying that he would be there each Sunday, but so far he hadn't stepped foot in the door. She prayed that he was a Christian as he'd told the children he was. For his sake, for their sake, and for . . . Beth shook the next thought out of her head. She'd have to see what he did on Sunday.

She made herself a cup of tea and took it over into the connecting parlor. She sat in her favorite chair, a worn rocker of her aunt's, and took a sip from the cup . . . thinking back on the past month since Jeb had come into their lives. Her opinion of him had changed so drastically since their first meeting. Beth had become accustomed to his company and enjoyed having him around . . . and she missed him when he wasn't. Which wasn't altogether a good thing. When he decided to leave, she would miss him even more. And so would the children. They loved him more each day. He was so good with them — and to them. What would they do if he decided the responsibility was too much and that he couldn't stay in one place?

Yet he seemed to be happy here — to love being around Cassie and Lucas as much as they loved being around him. Surely he would stay. But all she kept remembering was Harland telling her that he'd tried to get Jeb to settle down near him and Mary many times before she died, and Jeb would have none of it, saying there was just too much country to see, too many things he wanted to do.

She didn't want to see the children heartbroken. They'd been through so much as it was. Beth bent her head in prayer. *Oh, dear Lord, please let Jeb decide to stay for Cas-*

sie and Lucas's sake. They need family, and they need stability in their lives. Please, please, let their love and the ranch be enough to make Jeb want to stay here. In Jesus' name I pray, amen.

In another month it would be Thanksgiving. He seemed almost as excited as Cassie and Lucas about it — about spending it with them. But would he still be here then? A month after that would come Christmas. Would he stay to finish the house? And if he did, would he remember his proposal? He'd mentioned nothing more of it to her. Beth sighed deeply and took a long drink of her tea. Deep inside her heart, she was disappointed that he hadn't.

CHAPTER 7

Beth tried not to show the deep disappointment she felt that Jeb hadn't shown up to go to church with them. She'd had a hard time convincing the children that they couldn't wait any longer for him. In desperation, she'd kept their hope alive by suggesting that he might already be at church waiting for them. She tried to tamp down the anger she felt that he hadn't kept his word to Cassie and Lucas as they settled themselves in their usual pew, halfway up the aisle, on Sunday morning.

Still, Lucas kept craning his neck to watch for his uncle Jeb, and Beth didn't have the heart to tell him his uncle probably wouldn't show up. They were well into singing the second hymn of the morning when Lucas tugged at her skirt.

"He's here!" he whispered loudly.

Beth's head wasn't the only one that turned at his words. She peeked around Lu-

133

cas to see Jeb Winslow, standing there in the door of the church, obviously looking for them. Her heart did a flip-flop down into her stomach and back up again as he spotted them and made his way down the aisle.

She and Cassie moved down to make room for him at the end of the pew, and Lucas handed him his hymnal. Beth quickly blinked back the tears that formed behind her eyes, telling herself that it was the look of joy on the faces of Cassie and Lucas that caused them. But she was totally aware that she was every bit as happy as they were.

When Jeb lifted his voice in song, her heart made music to match his beautiful tenor, and she began to sing "Amazing Grace" with a thankful heart.

Beth was totally aware of Jeb's bowed head as prayers were said, of the attention he gave to Minister Turley's sermon, flipping through the worn Bible he'd brought with him to find the verses the minister pointed out. Her heart soared with joy, and she sent up her own silent prayer of thanksgiving that Jeb had shown up and that she finally knew that he was a Christian.

But her joy was short-lived when she realized that didn't mean he would settle here for the rest of his life. Harland had been so convinced his brother could never stay in one spot for long. And even though he'd already claimed a large portion of her heart, she just couldn't allow herself to care more for him. How could she ever trust that he would stay? Jeb could still decide that staying in the Roswell area wasn't for him and feel the need to move on, leaving the children with her, all of them alone. Worse yet, he might take them with him, leaving her alone. And totally heartbroken. She could only pray that didn't happen.

When the service was over, Beth realized her thoughts had been anywhere but where they should have been — focused on Minister Turley's sermon. She sent up a silent prayer, asking forgiveness as she went down the aisle with Jeb and the children. It was slow going as first one person, then another stopped them to welcome Jeb.

The Johnsons and the McAllisters welcomed him like an old friend and waited patiently behind them as Mrs. Alma waited for an introduction.

" 'Bout time you made it to church, young man," she said to Jeb once Beth had introduced them.

"Yes, ma'am. I suppose it is," Jeb admitted with a smile.

"Well, we're glad to have you here."

"Thank you. It's good to be here, Mrs.

Burton."

"See you come again," Alma instructed, with a short nod to emphasize her words.

"Yes, ma'am. I will," Jeb answered respectfully. Beth's heart warmed at the way he responded to the old woman.

Beth introduced him to Darcie and her mother, Molly Malone, to Jed and Laura Brewster, and to Miss Harriet Howard, one of Alma's friends, on their way to the door where Minister Turley waited to greet him.

The minister shook hands with Jeb. "Good to see you here, Mr. Winslow."

"Good to be here. Please, just call me Jeb, though."

Minister Turley nodded. "Jeb, I hope we'll see you again next week."

"Yes, sir, you will. I haven't always lived near enough to a church to hear many sermons, but I sure did enjoy yours today."

"Thank you. That's always a pleasure to hear."

"Uncle Jeb has been talking to God while he rides his horse," Lucas informed the minister from behind his uncle.

"Well, I'm of the opinion that we can talk to the Lord anyplace we are," the minister responded, with a smile. "Main thing is that we talk to Him."

Jeb nodded. "That's what I figure, too.

And I'll keep right on doing that. But it's good to have a church close enough to enjoy the fellowship of others."

"It sure is," Matt agreed, giving Jeb a friendly slap on the back.

The group continued down the church steps and into the yard. "And speaking of fellowship," Matt continued, "Emma and I would like to ask you all to come over to the café for Sunday dinner. The McAllisters will be there, too."

"Whatever you want to do is fine with me," Jeb assured her.

She glanced at Cassie and Lucas and could tell they wanted her to say yes. She'd planned on roasting a hen, but she could do that the next night. At the moment, her emotions were in turmoil . . . thrilled that Jeb had come to church, that he trusted in Jesus as his Savior . . . just as she'd prayed about. And yet unable to trust that he would stay put, how could she ever give her heart to him?

It might be easier to spend the day with Jeb if mutual friends were around. She smiled and nodded at Matt and Emma. "That would be wonderful. Thank you for the invitation. What can I bring?"

"Just yourselves. Liddy brought some pies, and I have a very large ham baking. Just come on down whenever you want."

"We'll be there soon. At least I can help you finish it up and get it on the table."

"I'll take you all to Emma's. I brought the wagon," Jeb announced to Beth. "I'd meant to get into town early enough to bring you to church, but I never asked what time the service started."

He helped her up onto the seat while the children hurried to sit at the back of the wagon, and Beth saw the bouquet of wildflowers lying on the floorboard. Jeb handed them to her when he took his seat. "My excuse for being late. I passed a field of these on the way into town, and you liked the last ones we picked so well . . ."

Beth's heart melted, and she didn't know what to say except, "Thank you, Jeb."

"I'd meant to get them to you before church so you could put them in water. They're beginning to look a little limp."

"They are beautiful, Jeb." Hoping to hide just how very touched she was by his thoughtfulness, Beth brought them close to her face and inhaled the sweet scent of the blooms. No one had ever brought her flowers until Jeb did. Not even Harland. The fact that Jeb had been so thoughtful made her want to cry for some reason. Why did he have to be so thoughtful? She blinked quickly and chewed her bottom lip for a moment as she held the bouquet to her chest.

"If you don't mind, would you stop by the house so that I can put them in water?"

Jeb smiled. "I'd be glad to."

Beth noticed several couples watching them as Jeb turned the wagon out of the churchyard and started down the road, and she had a feeling they'd be the talk of the town very soon. She could just see the switchboard lighting up, with people hurrying to spread the word that Jeb had come to church and was taking them home. Oh, yes. If she didn't miss her guess, they would be the topic of conversation all afternoon.

Jeb wished he'd made it into town in time to pick Beth, Luke, and Cassie up for church. It had been a little embarrassing to stand there in the doorway looking for them, but the happiness on the children's faces had been worth more than any momentary discomfort he'd felt. And once the service was over, everyone had made him feel right at home. There were some really nice folks in this area. But the people responsible for making him want to think about settling down were sitting right here in the wagon with him.

Beth was lovely in a blue suit with gold-braided trim of some sort and a dainty hat of the same color atop her head. But she was truly beautiful on the inside, where it counted most.

He wanted to show her the plans Michael Snow had given him — to see if there were any suggestions she might have. But he wasn't sure how to go about it. He didn't want to risk having her think he felt assured that she would marry him when the house was finished. Nothing could be farther from the truth. He thought she was beginning to care about him, but it hadn't been that long since she'd been planning on walking down the aisle with his brother — even if she hadn't known him very well.

Jeb wasn't sure he could ever take his brother's place in her heart. It might well take more time than the few weeks left until Christmas to do that. He was determined to have the house finished by then . . . if the good Lord willed it so. And he was going to ask her to marry him again. But if she wasn't ready to commit to him then, he wasn't going to give up. Beth was a woman worth waiting for.

He pulled the wagon up to her door and helped her down from the wagon. He stood watching her hurry into the house, glad that he'd brought her the bouquet, sad as it was.

"She sure does like those flowers, doesn't she, Uncle Jeb?" Lucas asked.

"Yes, she sure does," Jeb agreed, grinning at his nephew. "Let that be a lesson for you, Lucas."

The young boy scratched his head. "What kind of lesson?"

"A life lesson in what a lady likes. It might come in handy one day when you are courting one."

"What does that mean?" Lucas asked.

Cassie giggled. "It means that you are trying to get her to like you enough to marry you, doesn't it, Uncle Jeb?"

"Something like that." Jeb grinned at his niece.

"Oh," Lucas squeaked. "Are you courting Miss Beth?"

"Well, I'm trying to . . . but don't tell her." Jeb figured he had already said more than his nephew needed to know.

"Why not?"

"It might not help my cause."

"What is your cause?" Lucas appeared really confused.

"Oh, Lucas! Never mind." Cassie rolled her eyes at him. "Just don't tell Miss Beth that Uncle Jeb is trying to court her."

Lucas shrugged and shook his head. "I

won't. I promise. I'm still not even sure what courting is."

"Neither am I. But thanks, Lucas." Jeb ruffled his hair and grinned at Cassie. "And thank you, Cassie."

"I sure hope it works, Uncle Jeb," she whispered, grinning back at him.

"So do I."

Beth came out of the house just then, and Lucas chuckled while Cassie nudged him and said, "Shhh."

Jeb helped Beth back up into the wagon, pleased at the smile she gave him.

"The flowers perked right up as soon as I put them in water. Thank you again."

"You're welcome." Jeb figured it might have been worth being late this morning, just to make her so happy. She sure did like flowers. He'd have to find a spot to plant some near the house so she could see them every day . . . should she ever consent to be his wife.

The McAllisters were at Emma's Café when they arrived, and Beth hurried to the kitchen to find Emma and Liddy dishing up the meal. Emma's Café was closed on Sundays, and Matt and Emma took advantage of it to have their friends over.

Several tables had been put together to

accommodate everyone, with a table set for the children nearby, and Liddy had put her girls to work setting them. Beth didn't have to ask Cassie to help, as she offered as soon as they got there. She couldn't be prouder of Harland's children if they were her very own.

But all the children were well behaved, and they all bowed their heads as Matt said a prayer before the meal. Beth helped Cassie fix her plate and Jeb helped Lucas . . . she couldn't help but notice that they seemed like a family just as Cal and Liddy did, helping their children settle down with their food, or Matt and Emma, as they debated whether to seat Mandy beside them or let the girls help with her.

"Oh, please let her sit with us," Cassie begged Emma. "Lucas and I will help with her, Mrs. Johnson."

Grace and Amy added that they would help, too, and in the end, Mandy did end up at the children's table, having the time of her life with all the attention.

"How is the house coming?" Matt asked Jeb as he dished up a huge slice of ham onto a plate and handed it to him.

"It's going pretty good. If the good weather holds, I think I'll have it finished by Christmas."

Beth's pulse sped up as Jeb smiled and handed her a basket of rolls. Would he ask her to marry him again? Dare she hope that he would? As their hands brushed against each other and her heart skipped several beats, Beth knew that she already did.

"Harland would be proud of what you're doing to the place," Cal commented. "He really had big plans for the ranch and the future. I'm sure he'd like what you are doing to the house."

Harland. The man she'd been going to marry. Beth hadn't really thought about him in days. She'd been too busy thinking about Jeb . . . coming to care too much for him. Surely she wasn't trying to replace one brother with another?

"Thank you," Jeb answered Cal. "I don't know all the plans he had, but I know a lot about cattle, and I've even helped put up a ranch building or two. I'm trying to do what I think he would have done had he lived."

How could she care so much about Jeb now . . . when she couldn't learn to love his brother, whom she'd promised to marry? And had he lived, would she have told him she couldn't marry him? That she didn't love him?

Beth couldn't sleep that night. She tossed

and turned, finally getting up an hour early to make a cup of tea, hoping it would take her mind off the guilt she felt that she couldn't get Jeb out of her mind long enough to think about his brother. The man she'd promised to wed.

She'd agreed to marry Harland, had been happy that he wanted to move to Roswell to start their life together. He was a good man. An honorable man. And yet . . . she had been thinking of breaking her promise to marry him.

Now here she was falling in love with his brother . . . and praying that he stayed around and asked her to marry him again. How could she be so disloyal to Harland's memory? No answers came to her, and she shook her head as she went to wake up the children and get ready for work.

By the time Beth got to the telephone office, her heart was heavy with the guilt she felt, and by the end of the day, she felt no better. Her switchboard had been lit up all day, but she'd made few connections. Most everyone wanted to talk to her . . . about Jeb.

Mrs. Alma was the first to comment. "That brother of Harland's seems a good man, Beth. You could do a lot worse than marry him."

"Why, Mrs. Alma! I —"

"It would solve all of your problems, Beth, dear. The children are his kin. You love them. The two of you could make a nice home for them."

"But, Mrs. Alma —"

"You just think about it. 'Nough said." With that, Alma hung up her receiver, and Beth disconnected her line.

Another one lit up. This time it was Doc Bradshaw's line.

"Number, please," Beth said.

It was Doc's wife, Myrtle. "Hello, Beth, dear. I just wanted to talk to you a minute. How are you today?"

"I'm just fine. And you?"

"Doin' good. And if I wasn't, Doc would set me to rights."

Beth chuckled. "That he would. What can I do for you?"

"Not a thing, dear. I just wanted to tell you what a nice-looking couple you and Mr. Winslow make."

"But we aren't a couple, Mrs. Doc." Myrtle refused to let anyone call her Mrs. Bradshaw. It was just too formal for her.

"Well, you should be, Beth."

Beth didn't know what to say. "I . . . well . . . I . . ."

Myrtle didn't seem to expect a reply. "I

have to go, dear. It was nice talking to you."

Beth sighed and shook her head as she disconnected the line. Didn't these women have anything better to do than try to be matchmakers?

By afternoon, she was almost afraid to see her switchboard light up. She'd never had so many sweet busybodies telling her what to do. During a momentary lull, she leaned back in her chair and rubbed the back of her neck.

"No, Mrs. Howard, this isn't Beth. She's working the other switchboard this morning." Darcie grinned over at Beth.

Beth watched as her friend listened to the woman on the other end of the line for a moment, nodding her unspoken agreement.

"I'll be sure and tell her," Darcie said before disconnecting the line. She chuckled and turned to Beth. "Mrs. Howard wants me to let you know that she thinks that you and Jeb and the children make a beautiful family . . . and you'd better snatch him up fast. Of course, I think the same thing."

Sudden tears sprang to Beth's eyes. "Oh, Darcie. How can I? He may not even stay. And even if he did, how could I be so disloyal to Harland as to fall in love with his brother?"

Darcie jumped up and hurried over to

Beth. "Oh, Beth. I'm sorry. I didn't mean to make you cry!" She pulled a clean handkerchief from her pocket and handed it to her.

Beth dabbed at her eyes and shook her head. "You didn't. It's me, don't you see?"

Darcie's switchboard lit up, and she rushed back to it, looking over at Beth. "It's not you. I think we need a cup of tea at Emma's after work. Don't you let everyone upset you so."

Her own switchboard lighting again, Beth composed herself the best she could and connected the line. "Number, please?"

"Get me the sheriff's office, will you?" Homer Williams, a barber and one of the town's councilmen, asked.

"Certainly, Mr. Williams." Beth breathed a sigh of relief that it wasn't someone else wanting to give her their advice and connected the lines.

The rest of the afternoon was busy enough that if a caller wanted to talk to Beth, she could honestly tell them she had another line to connect. Still she watched the clock and had never been more relieved than when Martha and Jessica came in to relieve her and Darcie.

"I called Emma and told her we were coming for tea," Darcie informed her as she

148

closed the office door behind them.

"Oh, Darcie. I'm all right now. There's no need —"

"Yes, there is. I told Mother I would be a little late getting home, and Cassie and Lucas don't get out of school for another hour. It's been a long time since we've gone to tea."

Darcie rarely took time for herself, and she was trying to make her feel better. Beth couldn't turn her down. "All right. Let's go."

The day was cooling fast, and they hurried down the boardwalk toward Emma's. She met them at the door.

"I've been watching for you. It's really chilly out there," Emma said. "Hallie is going to watch the front for me. And we are going upstairs. Mandy is down for a nap, and we'll have more privacy up there." She led them through the kitchen and up the stairs to her and Matt's apartment. A small table had already been set for tea, and Emma motioned for them to sit down. "I'm so glad Darcie suggested this. We haven't had a chance to just sit and talk in a long while."

Beth took a seat and smiled at her friend. "No, we haven't. And I know you both mean well, but this really isn't necessary. I

149

just . . . had too much advice this morning."

"Beth, we're your friends. And we aren't going to give you advice. But you seem to be upset, and we'd like to help you if we can." Emma sat down across from her and began to pour the tea.

Beth swallowed around the lump in her throat. She was blessed to have such caring friends. And she did need to talk . . . if for no other reason than to be honest with herself and them.

"I'm not sure I deserve your care."

"What makes you say that?" Emma asked.

"I'm just an awful person."

"Oh, Beth. That's the silliest thing I've ever heard you say," Darcie cried. "You are a wonderful person . . . look how you took in Harland's children, prepared to raise them as your own before Jeb was found."

Beth shook her head and stared into her cup. "I do love Cassie and Lucas. But . . . I didn't love their father . . . not the way I needed to, to marry him. I was going to tell him . . . but then he died before I had a chance to. And, as sorry as I was that he died . . ." Beth began to cry, and there was no stopping the tears that spilled over. "I . . . I was relieved that I didn't have to hurt him." She laid her head on the table and sobbed.

"Oh, dear Beth." Emma jumped up and hugged her while Darcie patted her hand. "I'm so sorry I wasn't more perceptive. I think anyone feeling the way you did would feel the same way. I really do. You didn't want to hurt him."

"But why didn't I care enough? And why do I care so much for Jeb when I —" Beth took a deep breath and pulled out the handkerchief that Darcie had given her earlier. She wiped her eyes. "Do you think I'm trying to replace one brother with another?"

"Of course not," Emma assured her. "Maybe if you *had* loved Harland and were grieving deeply over your loss, I suppose one might think that. But you just said you didn't love Harland, but you do care for Jeb. How would that be replacing one with the other?"

"I don't know. I just —"

"What is different about how you feel about Jeb, Beth?" Darcie asked.

Beth sighed. Everything was different. Her pulse never raced at just a glance from Harland the way it did when Jeb looked at her and smiled. And her heart never hammered in her chest when Harland was around as it did each time Jeb came near. "I — he — my heart —"

Emma chuckled and sat back down. "You know, you and Harland really didn't have much time to get to know each other before he died in that stampede, Beth. He didn't even come into town every day like Jeb does, did he?"

"No." Beth had always wondered how he could go several days without seeing the children, but she never questioned him about it. "He was so busy trying to get the herd together and the ranch started, he didn't get into town as often as Jeb."

"So you've really spent more time with Jeb, getting to know him, than you ever did with Harland," Darcie added.

Beth thought of all the evenings they'd spent having supper together, the hours he'd helped the children with their school-work or watched her and Cassie make pies. The day at the fair and picnics at the ranch . . . and poring over the Sears and Roebuck catalog together, getting to know each other's likes and dislikes. "That's true."

"I think it's very simple, Beth. You couldn't make yourself love Harland any more than you can keep yourself from caring about Jeb."

"It's all my fault for daring you to answer

that advertisement, Beth," Darcie exclaimed. "I am so sorry."

"It's not your fault, Darcie. I should never have taken the dare. But I thought we knew each other from our correspondence, and I truly thought it would all work out."

"You wanted to fall in love with Harland. I know you did," Emma said. "And I think you thought you loved him when he first arrived in Roswell. But it is hard to get to know someone just from a letter. And to tell you the truth, Beth, Matt and I never thought you and Harland made a very good match. He was a really good man, but he seemed too . . . too . . . stern, too serious . . . older than his years."

"I just feel so disloyal to him, the way I feel about Jeb." Beth expelled a deep breath. "It doesn't matter anyway. He may not stay. Harland was convinced that Jeb would never settle down, and I can't afford to let myself fall in love with him."

Emma glanced at Darcie, then back at Beth. Emma patted her hand. "Beth, dear. I think it's too late. I think you are already in love with the man."

Beth buried her head in her arms and cried in earnest.

CHAPTER 8

After her cry and the talk with Emma and Darcie, Beth felt decidedly better. Emma was right; it was too late. She did love Jeb, in spite of the fact that she was afraid he'd never stay in one spot. Even if he did stay, he'd never once mentioned his proposal again, and Beth wondered if he'd decided he didn't need her to help him raise the children.

Still, the children needed him in their lives, and she would pray that he stay and make a home for them, no matter how much she would miss them when they moved out to the ranch. They loved their uncle, and he obviously loved them. Surely he would stay for their sakes.

The next few weeks flew by, with Beth still receiving advice from just about everyone in town and trying not to think about it each time she saw Jeb.

One evening when he came for supper, he

brought the plans for the house for them to see. While it was hard to tell just what it would look like when he finished, it was going to be very nice. Beth could tell that much.

Jeb tried to explain as he pointed to one of the upstairs rooms. "This will be Cassie's bedroom, overlooking the apple orchard and the barn, and Lucas, this will be yours. It looks out over the barn and corral."

Lucas pointed at a larger room. "Is this yours, Uncle Jeb?"

"Mine and . . ." Jeb paused midsentence and glanced at Beth with a slight nod and a smile. "Yes, it will be mine."

"And what is this?" Cassie asked, pointing to one of the main rooms downstairs.

"That will be the front parlor." Jeb pointed to the room in back of it. "And this will be the back parlor. This is the dining room and, of course, here is the kitchen. In the dining room, I think I'll put up a plate rail."

As he talked about the kind of trim work and other finishing touches he'd like to make, Beth noticed that he seemed to have taken some of her suggestions to heart, and she couldn't help but be pleased. Still it didn't mean that he'd propose again . . . it didn't mean that at all.

Cassie and Lucas were obviously looking

forward to moving to the ranch, and Beth tried to be happy for them.

She refilled Jeb's coffee cup and her own. "Liddy telephoned me today. She'd like for us all to have Thanksgiving with them out at their place. She asked Matt and Emma, too. It sounded nice. I told her I would let her know. What would you all like to do?"

"Let's go!" Lucas shouted.

"I'd like to go. It will be fun to spend the day with Grace and Amy and Mandy," Cassie admitted.

"Anything is fine with me," Jeb assured her. "I like the McAllisters and the Johnsons."

Beth took a sip of coffee. "I'll accept the invitation, then, and ask her what I can bring."

Thanksgiving dawned sunny and cool. Beth was furnishing some of the desserts and was up early baking a three-layer chocolate cake, the apple pie she'd promised Lucas, and a pumpkin pie to go along with the cookies and bread pudding she'd made for Jeb the night before.

Cassie and Lucas could barely contain their excitement at spending the day out at Cal and Liddy's.

"When will Uncle Jeb be here?" Lucas

asked, looking out the window once again.

"He'll be here, soon, I'm sure," Beth replied as she packed the desserts into picnic baskets to take to Liddy's.

"What all do you think we'll be having for dinner?" Cassie asked.

"Well, roast turkey, I know. Liddy is doing that. I think Emma may be bringing a ham. And mashed potatoes, of course, and other vegetables."

"I'm getting hungry just thinking about it," Lucas said.

Beth took off her apron and brushed at the skirt of her nicest dress. It was a burgundy and pink stripe with a deep lace yoke. She'd dressed with care today, wanting to look her best. Truth be told, she was excited about spending the whole day with Jeb and the children. And it was an added bonus that they would be with good friends of hers.

"Here he is!" Lucas said. He quickly drew on his coat, opened the back door, and ran out to meet his uncle. Beth could hear Jeb chuckling as Lucas told him to hurry.

"Good morning," Jeb said on entering the kitchen. "My, don't you two ladies look pretty."

Cassie giggled, and Beth could feel herself blush at the compliment she'd been hoping for. "Thank you."

"It sure smells good in here."

"It's the cake Miss Beth just made." Lucas lifted the lid of the basket that held the cake so Jeb could see. "She makes the best chocolate cake in the whole world!"

Jeb sniffed appreciatively. "Are we sure we want to share this with everyone else? Maybe we should just stay here and eat cake?"

Lucas laughed and shook his head. "Then we'd miss out on the turkey and everything else!"

Jeb ruffled his nephew's hair. "I guess we'd better be on our way then — before I give in to the temptation to cut this cake."

Beth grinned at him as she quickly grabbed the handle of the basket. It was probably a good thing he didn't know about the bread pudding. "I best take charge of this basket then." She nodded toward the other baskets on the table. "You can bring those."

"What's in them?"

"Cookies and pumpkin pie and —" Cassie stopped in midsentence.

"Good things." Beth grinned and finished for her as the child realized she had come close to giving Jeb's surprise dessert away. She grabbed the basket it was in and handed it to Cassie. "Here, you are in charge of this one, dear." She leaned down and whispered, "See your uncle doesn't go snooping, okay?"

Cassie giggled and nodded.

Jeb took a basket in each hand and headed out the door. "Well, now. If I need a snack before we get there, a cookie will be easier to get to than a piece of cake anyway."

"Jeb Winslow! You wouldn't dare!"

He laughed all the way to the street, and by the time Beth made sure the children had their wraps on and got out to the wagon, he was munching quite happily on one of the cookies. Beth couldn't help but smile as he grinned at her. "Hard for me to resist a dare, Beth."

Beth understood perfectly. Oh, yes. After all, she'd answered that advertisement of Harland's on a dare. She chuckled and shook her head, thinking she could probably teach Jeb a thing or two about taking a dare.

Still, she couldn't stop herself from blushing or her stomach from fluttering as if a hundred butterflies had been released when she saw the look in his eye before he flipped the reins and headed toward the McAllisters'. Had he been referring to the challenge she'd given him about the house? Or was that just wishful thinking on her part?

■ ■ ■ ■

It was the best Thanksgiving Beth could remember in a long, long time. For several years after she moved to Roswell, it had been just her and Aunt Gertrude. Before that, her Thanksgivings were spent with just her and her parents and rarely anyone else.

But spending this one with Cassie, Lucas, Jeb, and her best friends was something she would never forget. Liddy and Emma kept bumping into each other while they finished preparing the meal, laughing all the while. They dodged the children . . . and the men as well . . . as they all ran in and out of the kitchen to ask when everything would be ready. Beth just couldn't imagine having a better time.

Liddy's dining room was filled to over-flowing, but no one seemed to mind as Cal said the prayer.

"Dear Lord, we thank You for this day and for the many blessings You've given us. We thank You for providing for us always. For our loved ones, for old friends and new. For this meal we are about to eat. And most especially for Your Son and our Savior, Jesus Christ. It is in His name that we pray. Amen."

"Amen," Jeb and Matt added at the same time.

Joy flooded Beth's soul knowing that Jeb was a Christian. She would always be comforted knowing that, whether he stayed or went. But she sent up a silent prayer that he would stay.

The meal was delicious, consisting of the roast turkey with stuffing, baked ham, mashed potatoes, squash, and onions in cream, cranberry jelly, and breadsticks. There were nuts and cheese and crackers along with the desserts that Liddy and Beth had brought.

Beth would never forget the look on Jeb's face as she served him a portion of her bread pudding.

He gazed up at her with a grin. "You made it for me?"

She could feel the color creep up her neck, feeling everyone's gaze on them, but she only nodded and waited while he dipped his fork into it and took a bite.

Jeb closed his eyes as if to savor the taste, swallowed, then he gave her a huge smile. "It's even better than I remember my mother's being. Thank you, Beth."

"You're welcome." Her heart flooded with warmth when he asked for seconds a few minutes later. How good it felt to make him happy!

After eating so much, none of the adults had the energy to do much of anything except to play some checkers, watch the children at play, and visit for most of the afternoon.

For the next few days, Jeb smiled every time he thought of Thanksgiving. He had to have been young the last time he enjoyed a Thanksgiving quite so much. He'd forgotten how wonderful the day could be when shared with family and good friends. And hard as it was to know that his brother was gone, Jeb was thankful that he had family left in Cassie and Lucas.

They were the last of his kin, and he loved them. He'd come to love Harland's children more than he even imagined he could . . . and the woman who'd taken them in and cared for them as if they were hers.

For a little while Thanksgiving Day, it had felt as if he and Beth and Cassie and Lucas were a real family. And he hoped that they would be. Beth had captured his heart almost from the first minute he'd met her, that first day at her house, looking at him with apprehension while Lucas peeked out from behind her skirts. Getting to know

Beth and how much she cared about Cassie and Lucas made him realize that her uneasiness that day had been due to worry that he might take the children away from Roswell . . . and her.

Well, he would be taking them out to the ranch, but he hoped with all his heart that she would agree to be his wife and come with them. In the meantime, he was working as hard as he could to get the house finished by Christmas.

It was too cool for Cassie and Lucas to come out and help on Saturdays. He was still living in the barn, and the fireplaces in the house weren't ready for a fire yet. He hoped to have that done soon, but he decided not to bring the children out until it was completely finished. He could hardly wait to see their reaction when they saw all the changes he'd been making.

He hitched up the wagon and headed to town. He had a few supplies to pick up and an order to place for some fixtures for the house. He'd been poring over the Sears, Roebuck, and Company catalog, trying to make a list. He'd check the different mercantiles in town, and if he couldn't find what he wanted there, he'd place an order to Sears and Roebuck.

As he headed into town, he was on the

lookout for the few remaining patches of wildflowers. It'd been pretty cold lately and they were dying out fast, but he found a small clump just off the road and drove the wagon over to it. The pretty yellow flowers looked real cheery on the overcast day, and he was sure Beth would love them. He picked as many as were there and put them on the floor of the wagon.

He wondered if the seed catalog he'd ordered had come in. He'd check the post office while he was in town. He didn't know a thing about planting flowers, but he was sure that Liddy McAllister could tell him the best time to plant them so that they would be a surprise for Beth come spring.

He stopped at the post office on his way to the Jaffa-Prager Company. The catalog hadn't come in, but he did have a letter from his old boss, John Biglow. Figuring it was just an answer to the letter he'd sent the man, Jeb stuffed it in his jacket pocket to read later and went on to the mercantile. He put in his order, and Mr. Cormack promised he'd put a rush on it to see if they could get it here before Christmas.

Jeb loaded up the supplies he'd bought and put the bag of candy he'd picked up for Cassie and Lucas beside him on the wagon seat. He slapped the reins, and as if they knew right where they were supposed to go, his horses took off in the direction of Beth's place.

It was turning dark, and the light gray smoke curling up from Beth's stovepipe along with lights in her kitchen seemed to welcome him and put a glow in his heart. He gathered up the bouquet and hurried to the door, holding it behind him.

Cassie must have been looking for him, because she opened the door before he had a chance to knock. "Uncle Jeb . . . guess what we're having for supper?"

"What?" Jeb entered the kitchen and sniffed. The enticing aroma told him that Beth was making one of his favorite meals, but he let Cassie tell him.

"We're having pinto beans, fried potatoes, and corn bread," Cassie announced with a grin. It was one of her favorite meals, too.

Beth smiled from the stove. "Good evening, Jeb. We're having pork chops, too."

"Miss Beth spoils us, doesn't she?" Jeb asked, ruffling Lucas's hair.

"She sure does." Lucas motioned for Jeb to bend down so he could whisper to him. "We're having an apple pie, too."

"Apple pie?" Jeb whispered back. "I think Miss Beth deserves something special for that, don't you?"

Lucas and Cassie both nodded.

"Would you get a jar of water to put these in, Cassie?" Jeb asked, handing the flowers to Lucas.

It was warm in the kitchen, but Jeb couldn't miss the sudden profusion of color that flooded Beth's cheeks. He could tell she was pleased, and it made him happy that he'd taken the time to stop and pick the flowers for her.

"Thank you, Jeb. I thought all the flowers had died out by now."

"Most of them have . . . but I spotted these on the way in and thought you'd like them, even if they only last a day or two."

Beth stood on tiptoe and pulled a vase down from a shelf. "I found this the other day. It was one of Aunt Gertrude's. We rarely used it, and I'd forgotten about it."

"It looks a little fancy for wildflowers," Jeb commented.

"It's just right," Beth insisted, handing it to Cassie to fill with water.

Lucas placed the bouquet in the vase and handed it to Beth. She brought it to the table and set it in the center. "They are even more beautiful in the vase. I'm glad I found it."

Jeb was thankful that his brother had put a

woodstove in the small room in the barn where he'd been staying. Otherwise, he wasn't sure he could have stayed out at the ranch until the house was finished. The nights were getting really cold.

He added a few sticks of wood to the fire he'd started when he got back from Beth's and poured himself a cup of warmed-over coffee from what he'd made that morning. He grimaced. It sure didn't taste like Beth's.

It was getting to where he was dreading coming back to the ranch at night. Oh, he loved the place and was eager to get the house finished . . . but it was awful lonely here in his room in a corner of the barn, with the only sounds a snort from the horses or the wind blowing outside.

He pulled his lone chair close to the stove and drew out the letter he'd picked up at the post office earlier in the day.

Dear Jeb, Got your letter. Been thinking on things. I sure hate to lose a good man like you. I wanted to see if you'd be interested in becoming a foreman for me? Your niece and nephew would be welcome company for my children, and I'd furnish you with a house. Job is open now. Let me know what you decide. John Biglow.

Jeb had been thinking about settling down even before he'd received the news about

Harland . . . and a foreman job would have been exactly what he wanted. Especially one working for John Biglow. He was a good man to work for.

But now . . . he laid the letter down and shook his head. He'd found the place he wanted to settle down in . . . the place he wanted to call home. It was right here on this ranch with Beth and the children.

Even if Beth refused his proposal when the house was finished, he didn't think he could leave. That would mean taking the children away, because he couldn't imagine life without them now, and that was something he didn't think he could do. Not to Beth, not to Cassie and Lucas, and not to himself. But could he really stay if she said no? Would the pain of seeing her and not having her in his and the children's lives be too hard to bear? Jeb sighed. He really didn't know.

Still, he needed to answer John's letter. Jeb quickly penned an answer telling him that he couldn't give him a firm answer until after Christmas and that if he needed to fill the post, to go ahead . . . that he would understand.

Then Jeb turned to the only One who knew what the future held. He bowed his head and prayed.

"Dear Lord, I don't know what Beth will say when I ask her to marry me again . . . only You do. You know that I love her and that I want us to make a home for Cassie and Lucas. I pray that she feels the same way and will agree to marry me. But it's all in Your hands, Lord. I pray Your will be done. In Jesus' name. Amen."

Beth dressed with care on Saturday night. Jeb was taking them to Emma's Café for dinner as had become a habit in the last month or so . . . in spite of Beth's insistence that it wasn't necessary.

But Jeb felt it was. He told her that taking her and Cassie and Lucas to dinner once a week didn't seem much in the way of repaying her for the wonderful meals she managed to make for him and his niece and nephew after working at the telephone office all day.

Tired as she might be some days, Beth wouldn't have had it any other way. She'd come to love making dinner for them. The children were always appreciative, but Jeb even more so. She'd become so used to him being there, she knew she would be terribly lonesome once he moved the children to the ranch.

She always enjoyed the night out at Emma's, though. It had become a treat she looked forward to each week, and the children loved it. Sometimes, Matt and Emma and Mandy joined them, and sometimes it was just the four of them; but it didn't matter; it was an enjoyable evening either way. She was looking forward to this evening.

When she opened the door to Jeb, she was doubly glad she'd bought a new dress. It was black wool with a lace-trimmed bodice and a matching cape.

And from the way Jeb looked at her, she knew she'd made a good choice.

His gaze captured hers, and her breath caught in her throat as he commented, "You look lovely tonight, Beth."

"Thank you. So do you." And he did look quite nice in the new brown three-piece suit he'd worn to church last Sunday.

Cassie and Lucas came into the room right then, and Beth's heart warmed as Jeb made sure to tell them both how nice they looked, too.

"It's cold out. Be sure to wear your warmest wraps," Jeb instructed.

They bundled up and hurried out to the wagon, where Jeb's horses were stamping and snorting. It was a short trip to the café, but Beth was thankful for the warmth inside as they entered the establishment.

Emma and Matt did join them tonight as business was a little slow.

"When it gets this cold, most people stay in. I'm thankful to have friends like you . . . or I'd have to shut down," Emma said, as they all took a seat around the table.

Beth chuckled. "You know that's not true. I've heard many a person say that they'd rather come here than dine at either the Roswell Hotel or the Pauly."

"Still, I'm glad you all braved the cold and came in tonight. I have chicken and dumplings and an Irish stew to choose from. Either one will warm you up for the ride home."

The chicken and dumplings won out, and soon their food was dished up and served by Hallie. After Matt said the blessing, the table was quiet for a few minutes except for the clink of eating utensils against the dishes.

"This is wonderful, Emma," Beth said. "I wonder why someone else's cooking always tastes better than your own?"

"It does, doesn't it?" Emma agreed.

Beth thoroughly enjoyed the company as well as the break from her own cooking.

"Miss Beth, did you tell Mrs. Johnson

about the Christmas program?" Cassie asked.

"No, dear. I was just getting ready to. Have you heard about the Christmas program at school, Emma?"

Emma smiled and nodded in Cassie's direction as she answered Beth. "Yes, Liddy told me that Grace and Amy are very excited about it. And she said everyone is welcome to come. I'm looking forward to it."

"That's right. They mentioned it last night, but I forgot to ask you about it, Beth. I've never been to a Christmas program at school — or anywhere else for that matter," Jeb admitted. "They never did such programs when I was in school."

"They didn't?" Lucas asked, his eyes big and round as he gazed at his uncle.

Jeb shook his head. "No. They didn't."

Lucas grinned. "I've never been to one, either. This is my first year in school, you know."

"Yes, I know."

"You'll come, won't you, Uncle Jeb?"

"Of course I will. But what do they do at a Christmas program?"

Beth chuckled. "Well, I'm not sure. I've never been to one, either. But between Cassie and Lucas, I've found out that it's held at the school. They say there will be a big Christmas tree set up, and the children will decorate it with things they bring from home. Lucas and Cassie want to make a garland from popped corn. Family and friends are invited and asked to bring desserts. Someone . . . Minister Turley or the school principal will read about the birth of Jesus from the Bible. I think they will sing some Christmas carols they've learned at school, then I think everyone else will join in to sing some favorites. I'm not sure what all else. But they are very excited about it."

"You know, it's been a long time since I spent Christmas with family or even in a town. I'm kind of looking forward to it," Jeb said.

"So am I. It's all the children have been talking about."

Once they were finished eating, Emma told Cassie and Lucas that they could take Mandy upstairs to play. They didn't need to be asked twice. Matt lifted Mandy out of her high chair, and she led the children through the kitchen.

"She isn't a baby any longer, Emma."

"I know." Emma sighed deeply, then she looked into Matt's eyes and smiled.

He smiled back.

Emma continued, "Maybe one day . . .

next summer, she'll have a baby brother or sister to play with."

"That would be nice," Beth commented before she fully realized what Emma had said. Then she jumped up from her chair. "Emma, are you expecting?"

Matt's grin, which was ear to ear, told Beth before Emma did.

"I am."

Jeb congratulated Matt, while Beth rounded the table to hug her friend. "I'm so happy for you! Oh my! Oh my! What wonderful news."

"We are very happy about it, of course. Matt and I would like a large family."

"Will you still be able to run the café?" Beth asked.

"We'll see. It's been so much a part of my life, I'm not sure I can give it up. But I may need to. Matt and our children come first now."

Beth only nodded. She was happy for Emma and Matt. Truly she was.

Jeb took Beth and the children home, smiling at their chatter. They were so looking forward to Christmas. Once back at Beth's, she made some hot chocolate to warm up the children before bedtime and Jeb for his ride home in the cold.

Lucas and Cassie's excitement was contagious, and pretty soon they were all talking about what decorations they could make.

"I can get some cranberries from Jaffa-Prager . . . we could string some of them along with the popcorn," Beth suggested.

"Oh, that would be pretty. And even if some of the other children think of the same thing, a lot of garland will make the tree look pretty."

"I can help," Jeb volunteered. When Lucas seemed a little doubtful, he continued, "I can thread a needle and sew some. When you are out on the range by yourself, there are some things you have to learn to do."

"Well, we're going to have a lot to string, so we'll be more than glad to accept your help, Jeb," Beth said. "And maybe you can teach Lucas how to thread a needle. There are a few things boys need to learn to do."

Jeb grinned at Lucas and gave him a playful tap him under the chin. "I'll be glad to teach him a thing or two."

"Will you teach me to hunt? I'd like to learn to do that!"

"Yes. One of these days, I'll do that — if you learn to thread that needle."

Lucas giggled. "All right. I'll learn."

Jeb waited until the children had been sent off to bed before asking the question uppermost on his mind after all the talk about Christmas . . . well, the *second* uppermost question on his mind. He didn't think Beth was ready for his proposal just yet.

She poured him a second cup of hot chocolate and sat down across from him. "Thank you for dinner tonight. It was very enjoyable."

"I enjoyed it . . . and you deserved it." Jeb took a sip of the aromatic liquid before continuing. "I need to ask you something, Beth."

"Oh?" Beth paused and took a sip from her own cup. "What is it?"

"I don't know what to get the children for Christmas."

"Oh . . . well, I'm not sure, either."

"Have they mentioned anything?"

Beth shook her head. "Not really. There are some dolls at Jaffa-Prager that Cassie showed to me when we were in there, and Lucas mentioned something about an air rifle and a cap gun. I don't know what that is, but it seems to be one of the newest things. And I'm not sure he's old enough for either."

"Hmm. I'll have to think about that. I'll ask Cal and Matt what they think, too. All this is new to me . . . thinking about presents and such for children."

Beth smiled at him. "I know. For me, too. You know, Cal and Liddy can probably give us some ideas. They're old hands at this by now."

"That's a great idea. And by the time Emma and Matt need to know, we will be, too," Jeb said.

It was only after he'd taken his leave and was on his way to the ranch that he realized he'd implied they'd be a complete family by then. He didn't know whether he should be relieved or disappointed that Beth said nothing about his comment. She'd just ducked her head and took a sip of her chocolate — but not before he noticed she'd blushed once again.

He felt like she truly cared about him . . . and maybe he should be more obvious in his courting. Trouble was, he was afraid she would reject him outright, and he didn't want to chance it. But it wasn't long until Christmas, and that's when he'd told her he'd be through with the house and would ask her, again, to marry him. If the weather held, the house would be ready. And Jeb sure hoped Beth hadn't forgotten her challenge. He certainly hadn't.

CHAPTER 9

During the next week, Jeb finally moved into a corner of the house. The fireplaces had been cleaned, and he had plenty of wood chopped and stacked outside the door. It might not be finished, but it was a whole lot warmer than the barn, and he could put in an hour or two working on the house of an evening. With Christmas fast approaching, he was working as hard as he could to get everything finished.

He was still waiting for the last few items he'd ordered to come in, but everything was falling together nicely. Mr. Cormack had convinced him to put up that new tarpaper until the shingles came in, which he'd ordered to match those already on the roof. That had bought him time to get the inside of the house finished. The new shingles had arrived, and he'd picked them up today. He planned to start putting them up in the next few days. The house didn't even look the same as it had when Beth and the children first saw it, and he couldn't wait for them to see it.

The staircase was sturdy and beautiful. The damaged floorboards, upstairs and down, had been replaced or repaired and cleaned. As Jeb ambled across them now, they gleamed in the light of his lantern. He'd found he did need help installing the pocket doors in both parlors, and Cal had helped him. The wraparound porch had been shored up and, of a morning, he loved having coffee out there. He enjoyed walking around and looking out onto the orchard and the place he thought would make a good garden area.

There was a new sink in the kitchen, and he'd built a cupboard around it. He'd ordered the range Beth had pointed out as well as that nice worktable she wanted. He might be presuming too much, but even if she refused his proposal, he'd bought what the kitchen needed.

He still had some trim work to put up, but the house was near enough finished now that he was going to ask Beth to bring the children out for a picnic next Saturday. He wasn't sure whose reaction he was most eager to see . . . Lucas's and Cassie's . . . or Beth's.

He hadn't had time to get over to Cal and Liddy's to ask about their suggestions on what Cassie and Lucas might like for Christmas, but he'd ask Beth if she'd talked to them. Their excitement about Christmas and moving to the ranch was growing each and every day, and Jeb's was growing right along with them.

On Tuesday, he'd stopped by the post office before going to Beth's and found an answer to the letter he'd sent John Biglow. It was short and to the point.

Jeb,
  Job awaits you whenever you decide to take me up on the offer. The children can be schooled with mine, here on the ranch. Just let me know.

Sincerely,
John Biglow

Jeb knew what he wanted his answer to be. He wanted to be able to tell John that he was going to settle down right here on this ranch with a new wife. But that was in Beth and the Lord's hands. Whether he could stay if she turned him down . . . well, that remained to be seen.

Jeb had taken them to church the past

Sunday, and he was still coming in for supper, but he wasn't staying as long after dinner as usual, saying he needed to get back and do some work on the house.

Beth was beginning to be envious of the time he spent on that house! Of course, she wasn't that eager for him to have it finished. It would mean the children would move, and she was dreading being alone. She wanted to see what he'd been doing and how it was coming along, but he'd said he didn't want Cassie and Lucas out there until it was safe to do so.

She was trying hard to keep her mind off of Jeb and whether or not he would ask her to marry him again. But it was hard to do when she was bombarded by questions at work. Not only was she still getting advice about her relationship with Jeb, now she was being asked about what she thought of the house.

She kept telling everyone she hadn't seen it, but that wasn't good enough.

"Have you seen the house yet, Beth?" Alma Burton inquired.

"No, ma'am, I haven't."

"Well, when are you going to? I hear your young man is doing a wonderful job on it."

"He's not my young man, Mrs. Alma."

"Well, he should be."

"My switchboard is lighting up, Mrs. Alma. I have to go now." Beth disconnected the older woman's pin and connected with the Harrisons'.

"Number, please?"

"No number," Nelda Harrison said. "I just wanted to tell you that Jim and I drove past the Winslow place today, and we think the work Harland's brother is doing is wonderful."

"I haven't seen it yet."

"No? Well, you need to go out and see what he's done," Nelda advised. "You won't recognize the place."

Beth couldn't help but be curious about it. Even Liddy was impressed with what she could see from the road. When Beth called to ask for suggestions for Cassie and Lucas for Christmas, she mentioned it.

"Jeb is working really hard, Beth. It doesn't even look like the same place."

"I'm getting more and more curious, Liddy. Everyone is telling me that same thing. But . . . I guess I'll have to wait until Jeb is ready for us to see it."

"You could come to my place and pass by," Liddy suggested.

Beth giggled. "Now that's an idea. If he doesn't decide to ask us out soon, I may just take your suggestion."

It was getting a bit frustrating as more and more people asked what she thought about the house. She just couldn't tell them. She didn't know. Jeb hadn't offered to take them out, and she didn't feel quite right about just showing up with the children.

She was feeling a little testy when he came for supper that night. How could she tell him she wanted to see the house without reminding him of his proposal and the challenge she'd given him? Much as she wanted him to remember, she didn't want to be the one to bring it up, and she was beginning to think he'd forgotten all about it.

But she could be truthful. "The switchboard was lit up all day with people telling me how good the house is looking."

"Is it nearly finished, Uncle Jeb?" Cassie asked.

"Won't be long now." Jeb took a sip of coffee, and his gaze met Beth's over the rim of the cup. "I should have it finished right before Christmas."

"When are we going to get to see it?" Lucas asked.

"Well, I was thinking maybe you could come out and have a picnic on Saturday, if Beth doesn't mind bringing the food. The kitchen still isn't completely finished."

"Can we go, Miss Beth?" Cassie asked.

183

"Please!" Lucas added.

Well, finally. "Of course we can. I'll be glad to make a picnic lunch." At least when the next person asked her about the house, she'd be able to tell them she and the children would be seeing it on the weekend.

"I hope to be finishing the roof. Are you sure you don't mind bringing Cassie and Lucas out? I can come in and get you all."

"I know the way. We'll be fine. We'll be there around noon, if that's all right?"

"That sounds fine. I'm eager to see what you all think of it. And there are a few things I'd like to get your advice on."

All of the built-up irritation Beth had felt all day melted in a puddle at her feet. He wanted her advice about the house. Maybe that meant he was planning on asking her to marry him again. And maybe not. She couldn't let herself think about what it might mean. Beth jumped up to clear the table. She had to steer her thoughts into another direction. "I'm looking forward to seeing it."

"I'm glad I've had good weather," Jeb said. "Christmas will be here before we know it."

"It sure will be. And it will be time to decorate that tree at school. How about we string some popcorn and cranberries?"

184

"Sounds good to me." Jeb chuckled. "How about you, Lucas? You ready to learn how to thread a needle?"

Cassie ran to get Beth's sewing basket while Jeb and Lucas popped the corn. Then Beth brought out the cranberries she'd found at Jaffa-Prager, and they began making garland.

It took only a moment to teach Lucas what to do, and for the next few hours, they took turns stringing and eating the popped corn. By the time the popcorn was gone, they found that the cranberry garland was longer by at least half, but they had two beautiful contributions to the decorating of the school tree.

"Next time, I'll have to pop more," Beth commented as she began to clean up. "I think it's time for bed, children. You have school tomorrow."

Jeb got to his feet. "Guess I'd better get back to the ranch."

Cassie and Lucas gave him a hug, and Beth walked him to the door.

"Did you ever get a chance to talk to Liddy about Christmas?" Jeb whispered.

Beth nodded and pulled a piece of paper from her pocket. "I telephoned her. These are some things she suggested."

"Thank you. I haven't had a chance to get

by their place. I guess I ought to see about getting one of those telephones installed. Can I get one out there?"

Beth nodded. "Yes, you're close to town, and there are lines out that way now. Cal and Liddy live farther out than you, and they have one. Would you like me to place your order tomorrow?"

"Would you, please? I've never had a use for one, but I suppose it would be good to have, once I move Cassie and Lucas out there."

"Well, naturally, I'm a big believer in having a telephone. Liddy and I can keep in touch much easier, instead of waiting to see each other on a Sunday or running into each other when she comes into town. Plus, if one of the children gets sick and you need a doctor to come out, it will make it easier and faster to get hold of him."

"I hadn't thought of all those things. Please, do put my order in tomorrow."

"I will."

Jeb stood looking at her for a moment. "You know . . . Christmas is almost here. The house is going to be finished soon."

Beth held her breath.

He reached out and touched a wayward curl of hair on her forehead. "You haven't forgotten your challenge to me, have you?"

She could only shake her head.

"Well, then . . . it appears you have some thinking to do. Because I haven't forgotten, either."

With that, he turned and ambled out the door, leaving Beth with her hand on her chest and a smile on her face.

Jeb came into town to have supper with them the next few nights, but he didn't mention anything else about the challenge or his proposal, and Beth was skittish as a newborn foal.

It appeared he really was going to stay in one spot, despite what Harland had said about him. He was a wonderful Christian man who loved Cassie and Lucas with all his heart. Beth knew he would raise them the way Harland would want them raised. And they loved him . . . as did she.

She could no longer deny that she'd fallen deeply, completely in love with the man. Deep down she felt he cared for her, too, and what she wanted most for Christmas was for him to ask her to marry him again. She knew what her answer would be.

By the time Saturday rolled around, Cassie and Lucas could barely contain their excitement about seeing the house. Beth kept them busy doing chores while she fried chicken and made the lunch they'd be taking out with them.

She'd made arrangements to rent a surrey from the livery, and it was delivered a little early, but Lucas thought that meant they should go ahead and go out to the ranch. Everything was ready, and Beth supposed Jeb wouldn't mind if they showed up a little earlier than planned. The children helped her load the picnic baskets, and they were on their way.

It was a beautiful, sunny day that had warmed up nicely. Still, it was cool enough for jackets. She was glad they'd be taking their picnic inside, but if the children were out moving around and playing, they'd be fine.

While Cassie and Lucas chattered to each other, Beth's thoughts were on Jeb and how wrong she'd been about him in the beginning. Maybe he had always moved from one ranch to another, and maybe he liked seeing other parts of the country, but what no one had taken into consideration was just how seriously Jeb took his responsibility or how much family meant to him, especially if they were now dependent on him.

"Oh, look how pretty it is," Cassie breathed as they rounded the bend in the road and the house came into view.

Beth reined in the horse so that they could get a good look. It truly didn't look like the same place. What had been a rundown and uncared-for house was now looking like a real home. And there, on top of the roof, with his back to the road, was Jeb, hammering the new shingles in place.

As Beth drove into the yard, Lucas yelled, "Uncle Jeb!"

Jeb turned and waved. "You're early."

"I'm sorry," Beth apologized. "The children couldn't wait any longer."

Jeb smiled. "No. It's all right. But I'd like to finish up this section. You can put the basket on the table in the kitchen. But wait for me to show you the upstairs, all right?"

"We'll wait," Beth agreed. He'd worked hard, and she could understand why he wanted to be with them when they saw the changes to the inside of the house for the first time. She and the children unloaded the baskets and took them inside.

Beth tried not to look too closely at anything as she headed for the kitchen. She couldn't help but notice that the stove had been removed, but there were new cupboards and a new sink. The trim work had been done, and with some curtains at the window and a nice worktable in the center, it would be a wonderful place to prepare meals. Beth slid the baskets onto the old table that Jeb had brought in from somewhere, and she hurried the children back outside, so as not to notice too many other changes until Jeb could point them out.

Lucas ran out into the yard and craned his neck to see his uncle. "Can I come up there and help, Uncle Jeb?" Lucas asked.

"I don't think that's a good idea, Lucas. It's pretty steep up here. But guess what's in the barn?"

"What?"

"Four new kittens. A tabby showed up a few nights ago and made herself right at home out there. This morning, I heard a tiny mewing sound and found she'd had babies during the night."

"Let's go, Cassie," Lucas shouted, taking off in a run.

"Don't pick them up . . . just look at them. I don't think the mama would take kindly to you holding her babies just yet."

"We'll only look, Uncle Jeb," Cassie promised, hurrying to catch up with her brother.

Jeb smiled down at Beth. "I only have a few more shingles that I brought up earlier. I'll be down soon. Don't you want to go see the kittens?"

I'd rather watch you. "No, I'm fine here on

the porch. The house looks beautiful from the road, Jeb. Everyone is right . . . you've done a wonderful job on the house."

"Thank you. I hope you like the inside as well." He picked up a shingle. "I'll be down soon."

Beth watched as he knelt back down on the roof and began to hammer again. Her heart filled to overflowing with the love she felt. Not only had he developed a loving relationship with his niece and nephew, making time to see them nearly every day, he'd also put in long hours taking care of the ranch and making the house more than just livable again.

It was only a few minutes before Jeb came down from the roof, and Beth called the children from the barn.

"Let me show you the rest of the house before we eat," Jeb suggested. He led them up the porch steps and around to the back of the house.

"Oh, Jeb, this is nice. And the view of the orchards and the pasture is beautiful."

"It is pretty, isn't it?" He pointed to the side yard close to the kitchen. "I think that might make a good place for a kitchen garden. What do you think? Would you like that?"

Beth only nodded, not sure what to say.

She'd always wanted a garden similar to Liddy's . . . one big enough to feed a family. Still, there was something about the way he'd looked at her that had her heart pumping in her chest, and she could feel the flush on her face as she let herself daydream about the future.

She suddenly realized she was alone on the porch, and, flustered, she hurried into the kitchen where Jeb and the children were already washing up with the water Jeb was pumping into the sink. "The stove didn't work, so I've ordered a new one . . . but I added a few cupboards and cleaned out the root cellar."

"It's going to be a wonderful kitchen, Jeb," Beth said. She could just picture it all finished. "You did a really wonderful job on the cupboards, too."

"Thanks. There is still a lot to do, but once the roof is finished, it will be almost livable."

"It looks pretty livable already," Beth commented. "It just needs some furnishings."

Jeb nodded. "I have some of those ordered."

He pointed out the new plate rails he'd put up as they went through the dining room. The front parlor was much the same, but the broken windows had been replaced. As they started up the stairs, Beth couldn't help but notice how beautiful they were, as well as sturdy.

Cassie and Lucas ran on ahead of them, finding the rooms Jeb had pointed out to them from the house plans.

"This is mine!" Cassie exclaimed. "It looks out onto the orchard. Oh, Uncle Jeb, I love it!"

"And here is mine." Lucas ran into the opposite room and over to the window. "I wonder if I can see the animals in the barn from here."

Jeb sauntered up behind him and placed his hands on the young boy's shoulders. "Probably not unless they come out of it."

"I like it, Uncle Jeb!" Lucas pointed outside. "And look, I can see a couple of horses in the corral."

"I thought you might like this view."

"When are we going to move out here?"

Beth felt a twinge in her chest. What if Jeb didn't ask her to marry him? It was going to be so lonesome. Yet, he'd told her he hadn't forgotten. Surely . . .

"Sometime around Christmas if all goes well and the weather cooperates," Jeb answered. "I've been praying it does."

"I will, too," Lucas said.

"May we see your room, Uncle Jeb?" Cassie asked.

Jeb's gaze met Beth's for a moment. "Of course."

This room was much larger than the others . . . with two windows. One looked toward town and the other had a view of the orchard.

"Oh, this is nice," Beth couldn't help commenting.

"Well, up here is where I need some advice — and in the dining room and parlor, too. At the mercantile, they told me wallpaper would make it look really nice, but I don't know a thing about wall coverings — what to choose or anything. I was wondering if you could help me pick out some."

Beth glanced around the room and nodded. "Oh, that would be a nice touch. I'd be glad to help."

"Oh, I like wallpaper. It's so pretty," Cassie said. "Miss Emma has some in her apartment above the café."

Jeb grinned. "I feel better already, knowing that decorating stuff is left in someone else's hands."

Lucas was getting restless. "Can we eat now? I'm hungry. And may we go see the kittens again after lunch?"

"We'll see," Jeb answered. "First things

first. Let's go eat that nice picnic Beth made us."

The indoor picnic was a huge success. Jeb stirred to life the coals in the dining room fireplace and added a log. Beth laid the quilt she'd brought on the floor, and the children helped lay out the food and eating utensils.

"This room is so pretty, Jeb. With a nice table and sideboard, it will be a wonderful place to have meals in. I really like the plate rail, too." She could see the table set for company and almost hear the conversation. There was something about this room she just loved.

His gaze swept the room and he nodded. "It is nice. I think the Nordstroms had great plans for this house."

"And you've carried a lot of them out, I'm sure. It's gone from near ruin to a showplace in just a few months."

"Thank you," Jeb replied, finishing the large piece of pie Beth had cut for him. "I thought I'd follow you and the children back to town and we could go to Emma's tonight, but if it's all right with you, I'd like to get a few more shingles on this afternoon before we go in. Maybe, while the children are inspecting those kittens again and exploring the barn, you could go through the house and think about what kind of wallpaper might look good?"

"I'll be glad to do that. I'll clean up a bit; then I'll look around the house again and think about what you might like."

Jeb shrugged. "Anything you pick out will be fine with me."

He and the children went outside, and Beth began to clean up the picnic. After she'd packed everything to take back into town, she went back upstairs and surveyed the rooms. Cassie would probably like a wall covering with pink or lilac flowers in it, as those were her favorite colors. Beth wasn't sure about Lucas. Maybe a stripe of some kind would work. His favorite color was blue.

The small room would make a nice sewing room . . . or nursery. Beth shook off that thought for the moment, backing out into the hall and hurrying into the larger room. Although Jeb had hinted that he was going to ask her to marry him again, he hadn't brought it up since, and she needn't be thinking about nurseries until he did.

She walked over to the window of his room and looked out on the apple orchard. It was a wonderful room, sunny and bright. It would be hers, too, when and *if* — Jeb ever got around to proposing again. Was he ever going to? She just didn't know.

Beth shook her head and sighed as she headed back downstairs. Maybe the decisions on that room should wait until . . . well, they should just wait for now.

Beth decided to straighten and clean a bit until it was time to go back to town. There were little things she knew that Jeb might not think to get to right away. She swept the new floors, wiped down the windowsills, and cleaned the windows, polishing them until they shone. She dusted the fireplace mantels and was just finishing the last one when a folded piece of paper drifted to the floor. Beth picked it up, wondering if it had been here for long.

It hadn't. It was a short note . . . from Jeb's boss . . . telling him his job was open and the children were welcome. Beth's heart twisted in her chest. Was Harland right? Was Jeb fixing up the house only to sell out and go back North?

Well, there was only one way to find out. Beth ran though the house, down the porch steps, and around to the ladder leading to the roof. She clambered up it as fast as she could in her long skirts and holding the offending letter in her hand.

Jeb's back was to her when her head cleared the roof line. "Can you tell me the meaning of this, Jeb Winslow?"

"Beth?" Jeb whirled around. "The meaning of what? What's wrong?"

She waved the paper in her hand. "This is wrong! Have you been planning on taking this man up on his offer? Are you leaving here? Fixing up the house just to sell out? Are you taking the children with you?"

Jeb got to his feet and stared down at her . . . his mouth opening and shutting at first. Then he found his voice. "How could you think that? I just asked you to help me decorate this house! Why would I be working this hard . . . trying to get this roof finished before the first snow . . . the house ready before Christmas . . . if I didn't plan on making a home here?"

"You said that Mr. Snow thought it would add more value to the property!"

Jeb shut his eyes and shook his head before meeting her gaze again. "Beth Morgan — can't you see . . . I'm trying my best to get this house finished by Christmas to answer your challenge. And *why* would I be doing that?"

"I don't know. Why?"

"Because I —" Just as the words were out of his mouth, Jeb slipped and started sliding down the roof.

"Jeb!" Beth yelled, but there was nothing

she could do except watch him fall. She didn't know if she heard or felt the thud as he hit the ground, but her heart seemed to stop beating as she saw him lying on the ground. Jeb didn't move. *No!* Tears streamed down her face. It was all her fault. Had she killed the only man she'd ever loved?

CHAPTER 10

Beth backed down the ladder as fast as she could, totally missing the last rung and jumping to the ground. She hurried to his side and knelt down, feeling for a pulse. "Jeb! Jeb!

"Oh, please, dear Lord — let him be all right. Please. Please. He's such a good man, and the children need him. I need him. Dear Lord, please let him come to."

She felt a faint pulse just as Jeb moaned, and Beth expelled the breath she didn't know she'd been holding. "Thank You, dear Lord. Thank You!"

Another moan assured her Jeb was alive but hurting. "Cassie! Lucas! Bring the wagon over here. Come quickly!"

The children came running. "Uncle Jeb! Is he going to be all right, Miss Beth?"

"I hope so, Cassie. We need to get him into town to the doctor."

Jeb opened his eyes and grimaced. "I'll be

fine. Had the air knocked out of me. Just help me up from here."

"Lie still," Beth instructed as she noticed one arm seemed to twist at an odd angle. She gently touched it. He winced and groaned again. "Jeb, you're hurt. We need to get you to Doc's."

"Let me just . . ." Jeb put his other hand on the ground and tried to lift himself up, trying to get to his knees. "Arrgh!" Sweat broke out on his brow, but he managed a smile for Lucas, who was openly crying.

"I'm going to be fine, Lucas. Guess I should have had one of those telephones put in earlier."

"We'll get you some help," Beth promised. "Cassie, come get your arm up under your uncle Jeb's other arm. I'll try not to hurt this one any more than is necessary, Jeb."

He nodded, and Beth could tell he was gritting his teeth as they got him to his feet. Beth knew afterward that it was only with the Lord's help that they were able to get him into the wagon at all. He weighed more than she and Cassie together.

She lost no time getting him back to town. Thankfully, Doc Bradshaw's office was attached to his home, and before Beth got the wagon to a full stop, Lucas was up the walk and pounding on the door.

"What is it? What is it?" Doc asked, opening the door.

"Uncle Jeb fell off the roof of the house, and he's hurt real bad."

"Myrtle, call the sheriff's office and get someone over here to help me get Jeb in the office," Doc yelled back into the house. He hurried to the wagon to find Jeb had passed out.

"Is he all right?" Beth asked, wiping her eyes yet again.

"He's alive," Doc said. "All the jostling around most likely was just too much for him and he passed out. Tell me what happened."

"Well, we were . . ." How could she tell Doc that they were yelling at each other?

"Uncle Jeb was working on the roof of the house and he slipped off of it," Cassie informed Doc.

Beth sent up a silent prayer of thanksgiving that the children had been in the barn and hadn't heard her tirade. "I think his arm is hurt bad . . . and I'm not sure what else. I just know he's in a lot of pain."

Matt came running up just then. "What do you need, Doc?"

"Help me get Jeb into the office so I can examine him."

Matt took a look at Jeb, then back at Beth

202

and the children. "Why don't you go over to the café and wait with Emma? I'll come get you soon as Doc has Jeb settled."

"But I —"

"It might be better for the children, Beth," Matt suggested, inclining his head in their direction.

Beth turned to Cassie and Lucas. The fear on their faces was obvious for anyone to see. Beth nodded. "Cassie, Lucas, let's go to see Emma. Your uncle is going to be fine. Doc will see to it."

Doc nodded. "I'll get word to you, soon as I examine him and get him comfortable."

When Lucas hung back, Doc bent down and looked him in the eye. "Lucas, I promise your uncle is going to be all right."

Only then did the young boy slip his hand into Beth's and let her lead him across the street to Emma's Café.

Emma met them at the door, Mandy in her arms. "Myrtle telephoned me and told me you were on your way here."

"Uncle Jeb is hurt real bad," Lucas told Emma. Cassie was unnaturally quiet.

Emma nodded. "But, you know, Doc is real good about helping people, and we're going to pray that your uncle Jeb gets well real soon."

"Can we pray now?" Cassie asked.

"Yes, we can," Beth answered.

And there, in the doorway of Emma's Café, huddled in a tight circle, they did just that.

Emma suggested they all go up to her apartment so that Mandy could help occupy the children's minds and she and Beth could talk. She brewed a pot of tea for her, and Beth then settled the children at the table with some molasses cookies and milk.

Mandy had Cassie and Lucas laughing in spite of their worry over their uncle, and Beth was glad Matt had suggested that she bring them here.

She and Emma took their tea to a small table in the parlor. Beth took a sip from her cup and let out a deep breath.

"He'll be all right, Beth," Emma tried to assure her.

"I pray so." Tears sprung to her eyes again. "It was all my fault, Em."

"What was?"

"Jeb's fall. We were yelling at each other —"

"Yelling? You and Jeb?"

Beth nodded and sniffed. "I found a letter, and I thought it meant he was going to leave . . . and I climbed the ladder and confronted him about it."

"What did he say?"

"Before he fell off the roof?"

Emma nodded.

Beth sniffed and tears began to fall again. "He . . . got angry and was trying to tell me I was wrong when he . . . when he slipped and fell off the roof!" With that, she began to sob.

Emma jumped up and came around to hug her. "Oh, Beth. It's going to be all right. Did you hear what you just said? Jeb was telling you that you were wrong. Probably was going to say he's staying. It's all going to work out for you, you'll see."

"Oh, Em. How can it? Because of me, he's hurt really bad . . . and could have died! How will he ever forgive me for that?"

"I'm sure he already has. Beth, he slipped. You didn't push him. He knows that."

Beth rocked herself back and forth. "It doesn't matter now. I just want him to be all right."

"He will be," Emma tried to reassure her.

Beth could only pray she was right as she watched the clock. The afternoon seemed much longer than the hour or so later when Matt finally telephoned Emma to let them know they could see Jeb. Beth and the children threw on their jackets and hurried back over to Doc Bradshaw's office as fast as they could.

"He's going to be fine, dear," Myrtle said as soon as she let them in. She led them to a room just down from Doc's examination room.

Doc came out of the room just then and smiled at Cassie and Lucas. "Your uncle is going to be just fine. He's awfully bruised and battered — may have a cracked rib, and he has a broken arm. He must have landed on it, and it's broke in several places. It will take awhile for it to heal." Doc patted Lucas on the head. "It *will* heal, but he isn't going to be able to climb up any ladders or pound any nails for a while to come. I'm going to keep him here for a few days to make sure that no infection develops, but you can come see him anytime."

"Can we see him now?" Lucas asked.

"Yes, you can. He's been asking to see you. But he'll be getting groggy from the medicine I gave him soon, so if he drifts off on you, don't worry."

"I won't," Lucas promised. He slipped his hand into Cassie's, and they waited for Beth.

"Thank you, Doc." Beth took Lucas's other hand and led the children in to see their uncle.

Although his broken arm was in a sling,

Beth was tremendously relieved to see that he appeared decidedly better than the last time they'd seen him. There was a little color to his face, and he smiled and motioned the children closer with his good arm. "Come here and see that I'm alive and well."

He managed to hug each one as Beth watched from the doorway. She didn't know what any of them would have done if he . . . if he . . .

"Beth?" Jeb was looking closely at her. "Are you all right? You look a little pale."

"I'm not the one who just fell off a roof. I'm glad you're going to be all right, Jeb. I'm sorry —"

"It was my fault," Jeb insisted, as if trying to reassure her. "I knew better than to stand up."

Beth shook her head. "No, it was my —"

"Beth. It was an accident."

"A bad one, too," Lucas responded with a wobbly voice. "I — I thought you were dead at first."

"So did I," Cassie said with a sniff.

Beth's gaze met Jeb's. In silent agreement, Jeb changed the subject.

"Well, as you can see . . . I'm alive and almost well." Jeb reached out with his good hand and tickled Lucas.

The child's laughter was the best sound Beth had heard since Jeb fell off the roof.

Beth was exhausted by the time she got the children settled down for the night, but she was still too upset to sleep.

Jeb had drifted off just as Doc had told them he would, and Beth and the children had tiptoed out of the room. Matt was waiting for them to take them back to the café. Emma had insisted that they come back over to her place for supper before going home, and Beth had to admit she was glad for the company. She didn't want to be alone with her thoughts.

But now in the quiet of the night, she could no longer avoid them. *Dear Father, please forgive me for losing my temper today, for causing Jeb to fall. For accusing him wrongly. Thank You for letting him be all right. Please help him to heal completely. And please help him to forgive me, too. In Jesus' name, amen.*

Beth didn't know how he could. Not only had she caused him to fall off the roof, she'd judged him on the basis of a piece of paper. She wouldn't blame him if he never wanted to talk to her again after he moved the children back to the ranch, even though it would break her heart if that was the case.

He was probably only being nice to her at Doc's because he didn't want to upset Cassie and Lucas. He was such a wonderful person. He'd been more concerned about his niece and nephew's fears than his own pain, assuring Cassie and Lucas that he would recover before he'd drifted off to sleep.

Oh, how she loved that man! Not that it would do her any good now. How could he possibly want to marry a woman whose awful tirade had caused him all the pain he was now enduring?

After a restless night, Beth got ready for church, resolved to do what she could to help Jeb get the house finished so he could move the children out to the ranch by Christmas. She telephoned Doc Bradshaw's to get a report on Jeb for the children. Myrtle told her he'd slept all night and that she was making a breakfast for him now.

Beth was relieved that he'd been able to sleep, and she asked Myrtle to tell Jeb she would bring Cassie and Lucas to see him after church.

Myrtle promised to do just that, telling Beth that she was sure that would make Jeb feel much better.

Word had certainly gotten around about

Jeb, which came as no surprise to Beth. Everyone she ran into asked her about him, and Minister Turley asked for prayers for his quick recovery. Cal and Liddy hurried up to her right after church, as did Emma and Matt, and Darcie and her mother.

"Emma called me last night and told me about Jeb, Beth," Liddy said. "Is there anything we can do?"

"Well, actually, I'm trying to figure out a way to get the roof finished for Jeb. He wanted to have it done by Christmas, but I don't see how he can do that now. Not with a broken arm and possible broken rib and being so bruised up. I was wondering —"

"Just leave it to Matt and me," Cal said. "We'll get a crew together and finish that roof in a day or two."

"I'll run over to the telephone office and have Jimmy Newland get the word out that you could use some help," Darcie suggested.

"That's a wonderful idea, Darcie," Matt commented. "How about asking any who are willing to meet us out at the Winslow place tomorrow morning?" He looked at Cal. "Will that work for you?"

Cal grinned and nodded. "I'll start asking around."

"Are we going to let Jeb in on this, or did

you just want to surprise him?" Cal asked Beth.

"Well, I'm afraid that if he knows, he'll think he has to be out there, too."

"You're right, he would. Let's just keep it quiet for now, then."

"Thank you all — I don't know what to say."

"No need to say anything. Jeb would do the same for us."

The next day, Beth kept busy at work and hurried home to take Cassie and Lucas to see Jeb when they got out of school. Thinking that she was probably the last person Jeb wanted to see, she tried to stay in the background . . . talking to Myrtle while the children visited with their uncle. Although he was not happy about being laid up, he was always glad to see his niece and nephew.

Beth longed to tell him about all the men who'd shown up to finish putting the shingles on the roof, but Doc advised her not to when she asked him about it.

"I'm having enough trouble keeping him here as it is, Beth. If he found out there were people working out at his place, he'd be impossible to keep down."

"That's what I thought, too, but —"

"Don't worry. If he wants to know why

you didn't tell him, I'll let him know I said not to."

"Thank you, Doc."

"You're welcome. Just be warned . . . he's a bit grouchy today."

Beth grinned and nodded. If he was grouchy to her . . . it was only what she deserved. She'd accept it. "I brought him some chicken and dumplings. Maybe that will perk him up."

"We can hope," Doc commented, heading back to his office.

"Where have you been?" Jeb asked as soon as she entered the room.

"I was talking to Doc. He says you are a bit . . . restless?"

Jeb shook his head. "I didn't mean just now . . . you haven't been — he said restless?"

Beth's heartbeat picked up in tempo. Had he missed her? "Well, his exact word might have been grouchy . . . but maybe it should have been both?"

"Well, how else would I be? I want to get that roof finished, and I'm not doing it in this bed."

"Jeb, I'm sorry —"

"Beth, we've been over that. I just want to get out of here and get back to the ranch."

"It won't be much longer."

"I keep thinking if I get ornery enough, Doc will kick me out of here," Jeb admitted.

"Uncle Jeb, you need to get well," Cassie responded.

Jeb sighed. "You're right, Cassie, love. I'm sorry. I'm not a very good patient, I'm afraid."

"Here." Beth handed him the bowl of dumplings and a spoon. "Emma sent you these. Maybe they'll make you feel better."

"They won't hurt none, that's for sure." Jeb grinned and dipped the spoon into the bowl. "Tell Emma thank you."

"I'll do that."

CHAPTER 11

By Tuesday, Jeb had been in bed just about as long as he could stand it. He'd had visitors and that helped. Matt and Emma had stopped by, and Cal had come by to tell him not to worry about his herd, he'd be watching out for it. But Beth seemed to be avoiding him, and it was time to get to the ranch. He wanted to get the house finished . . . if it was at all possible, by Christmas. Then she was going to have to face him.

Doc wasn't very happy about releasing him, but Jeb insisted. He was on his feet, his limp a little more prominent and his arm in a sling, but he was determined to go home — if he could find someone to take him.

"You are one stubborn man, Winslow." Doc Bradshaw shook his head. "You aren't going to be able to do much work out there. But there's no sign of infection in your arm, and it doesn't appear you broke any ribs. Your bruises seem to be healing well, so I guess I can't rightly keep you here forever."

"Doc, you can take me out, can't you? Or telephone Cal McAllister? I'm sure he'd come in and pick me up."

"I guess I'd be chomping at the bit to get back to my place, too, if I were you. I'll take you out there. You go on into the kitchen and have breakfast with Myrtle so she don't have to bring it to you, and I'll go get my surrey."

"Thanks, Doc . . . for patching me up and for puttin' up with my bad manners. I appreciate all you've done for me."

"Myrtle said you've been real nice to her. She thinks you are an exemplary patient." Doc rocked back on his heel as he motioned Jeb out of his room. "I guess you weren't too bad. Let's get you fed."

Doc followed him down the hall to the kitchen. "Look who's out of bed, Myrtle."

His wife turned from the stove where she was flipping pancakes. "Why, Jeb! Are you sure you feel well enough to be up and around?"

"He wouldn't tell you if he didn't, Myrtle. He's just determined to get back to the ranch. I'm going to get the surrey so's I can take him out there." He kissed his wife on the cheek before heading out the door. "Make sure he eats a good breakfast before I come back."

Myrtle did just that, piling Jeb's plate high with bacon, eggs, and the lightest pancakes he'd ever tasted. She poured his coffee and fussed over him until Doc came back. Jeb was going to miss all of her attention.

He kissed her on the cheek before he started toward the door. "Thank you for all the care you gave me, Mrs. Doc."

"You're welcome, Jeb. I wish all of Doc's patients were as good as you've been. You just try not to do too much, you hear?"

"Yes, ma'am, I do."

He limped out to the surrey, his body protesting with each step. It seemed to take forever, but he managed to get himself up onto the seat without bumping his bad arm. It appeared his battered body was going to hurt no matter what he did or didn't do.

"You sure about this?" Doc asked. "You ain't going to be able to do any work out there, you know."

"I've got a ranch to tend to, Doc. I can't just let it go."

Doc didn't say another word. He just shook his head, flicked the reins to his horse, and headed out of town.

Jeb was surprised at how badly he wanted

to be home and even more surprised that he'd found a place he wanted to call home. But he had. He'd come to love the ranch . . . the house as he worked on it, the land, and the animals. He wanted to make it something Harland would have been proud of. And deep down, Jeb knew that his brother would be overjoyed that he wanted to settle here.

The day was beautiful, but Jeb was painfully aware that he wasn't in any shape to climb up on the roof to finish those shingles. And he realized that if he was honest with himself, he probably wasn't going to meet the deadline that Beth had given him, either. Still, there were things inside the house that needed his attention, and he'd get done what he could.

When they came to the bend in the road, Jeb felt as if he'd been away much longer than a few days. He waited in anticipation for his first glimpse of the house when they rounded the curve.

"What in the world —" There on the roof of his house were Matt and several other men . . . and it was almost completely shingled. Cal and some others were coming and going from inside the house, too. Most of them he recognized from church . . . some he'd met and some he hadn't. He shook his head and turned to the doctor for an answer, "Doc, what's going on here?"

"Appears to me that your roof is getting shingled." Doc chuckled. "We've had a hard time keeping quiet about this."

"But how . . . why —"

"One thing led to another. Beth knew you wanted the roof shingled before bad weather came and that you wouldn't be able to do it yourself. She voiced her concern, and Cal and Matt decided to get a group together. From what I heard, word spread pretty quickly from the telephone office, and it took off from there." Doc pulled up into the yard.

"Jeb! Welcome home!" Matt yelled from the roof. He made his way down the ladder and started toward Jeb.

"Yeah, welcome home!" Cal added, crossing the yard toward them. "Doc, you let him go already?"

"I didn't have much choice. I think he would have walked, if he'd had to."

Jeb grinned and gingerly got out of the buggy. He turned to the men who'd come over to see how he was doing. "I don't know what to say 'cept thank you."

"Nothin' more needed," Cal said. "You'd do the same for us. We're 'bout through with the roof. But we've been busy inside, too. Mr. Cormack over at Jaffa-Prager heard you were down and that we were trying to help out. When your order came in, he telephoned me, and we told him to haul your stuff out here. We just got through setting your new range up. Come on and see if we did it right."

Jeb couldn't say anything. He was too busy swallowing around the lump in his throat. He'd never had people do anything like this for him. He'd be forever grateful to Matt and Cal . . . and all of these men who'd become his friends and accepted him as one of their own. He limped up the porch steps and went inside.

"That sure is some range you ordered." Cal cocked an eyebrow. "I didn't know you liked cooking that well."

Jeb laughed. "I was told it was a really great stove."

"Uh-huh. I wonder who might have mentioned it?"

"It's supposed to be new and improved." Jeb grinned and shrugged. "How does it look in the kitchen?"

"See for yourself. You barely had room on that wall for it. But we managed to get it in."

"Whoa," Jeb said when he saw it. "It is bigger than I realized." The Sterling Sunshine steel plate range was one of the largest he'd ever seen, with six holes and the water reservoir. But it sure did look pretty in the kitchen, and he couldn't wait for Beth to see it.

"Mr. Cormack says they come in different sizes, and this is about as big as it gets," Cal informed him.

"All I know is, Em is going to be jealous when she sees it." Matt leaned against the door facing. "I'll probably have to order her one."

"Yep. Same here," Cal agreed. "Probably ought to go ahead and do it."

Jeb just shrugged and laughed. Then he noticed the telephone. It was on the wall between the kitchen and the dining room. "When was this put up?"

"Yesterday afternoon. They said Beth told them someone would be here. We figured this would be the best place for it."

Jeb nodded. "Good. I guess I ought to let Beth know I'm back out here."

"Probably would be a good idea," Cal agreed.

"I don't know how to use it," Jeb admitted to his friends.

"It's easy," Matt assured him, walking over to the telephone. "Just pick up this black thing there on the hook and put it up to your ear. When someone from the telephone office says, 'Number, please,' you talk into this mouthpiece and tell them who you want to talk to."

"That's all there is to it?"

"That's it."

"I ought to be able to do that." Jeb wanted to telephone Beth, but he wasn't going to do it with all these men standing around. He would wait until they left the kitchen, then he'd try it. Maybe.

Matt and Cal exchanged a look and a grin. Matt nodded. "You'll figure it out."

"We're going to finish up those shingles while we have daylight."

"I really don't know how to thank you . . . all of you. If there is anything I can do —"

Cal laughed. "If you can figure out that fancy range, you could make us some coffee." He motioned to some crates on the worktable in the center of the kitchen. "There's some dishes and cooking things you ordered in those crates. We didn't know where to put them."

Jeb grinned. "Well, finally . . . something I should be able to handle. I'll call you when the coffee is made."

Beth heard about Jeb almost before he and Doc were out of town. Myrtle telephoned her to let her know that nothing would do for Jeb but to get back to the ranch.

"Doc took him out first thing this morning."

"How was he?" Beth chewed her bottom lip waiting for Myrtle to answer. He shouldn't be out there by himself. Surely he wouldn't try to —

"Well, not near as good as he'd like to be. But he'll be all right, dear. He's a sensible young man, and he's hurting more than he wants to admit. His body isn't going to let him do much. Besides, with all the men helping out there, he's not going to have to get back on that roof anytime soon."

"You're right, Myrtle." Beth prayed that she was. "I'm sure he will be fine out there." But her heart twisted at the thought that he was still in a lot of pain. And it was all her fault . . . and she knew it.

"Beth? Are you still there?"

"Yes, Myrtle, I am. Thanks for letting me know about Jeb."

"You're welcome, dear. Doc had a few stops he wanted to make on the way back in, but if there's any news I think you need to know, I'll get in touch with you."

"Thank you." Beth disconnected the line. Lucas and Cassie were going to be disappointed that they wouldn't see Jeb this

222

evening. Maybe they could go out . . . no. It was getting dark early, and Jeb would think he had to see them back to town. She couldn't have him doing that. His telephone had been installed. Maybe she could ring him. . . . No, she couldn't do that. What if he was upstairs and had to hurry to answer it? He could fall or hurt himself worse.

Beth sighed in frustration. Maybe she would just ring Emma and find out from Cal how he was when he left Jeb's. At least she'd know how he was then.

In the meantime, she was still getting all kinds of advice for Jeb, for her . . . and for them as a couple.

"When are you two going to get married? If you already were, he wouldn't be out there by himself," Alma commented.

And the likelihood of that happening has become a lot more unlikely since I caused Jeb's accident. But Beth didn't voice that to Alma. Instead, she just said, "I'm sure he will be fine. Doc wouldn't have let him go home if he didn't think he would be all right. Sorry, Mrs. Alma, I have to get busy."

And busy she stayed for the rest of the day, telling everyone who inquired about Jeb that he had gone back to the ranch and must be on the mend. And, yes, she and the children would be checking on him. And agreeing that she was sure he was quite surprised at the help the men had been giving him. And on and on and on.

Beth was relieved when it was time to go home but dreaded telling the children that they wouldn't be seeing their uncle Jeb. And they were disappointed. However, they were very pleased that Jeb was well enough to go back to the ranch.

"When do you think we'll get to see him, Miss Beth?"

"Well, I'm not sure he'll feel like riding a horse for a while or how hard it will be for him to hitch up the wagon. But if we don't see him by Saturday, I'll take you out there."

That seemed to satisfy them, but it didn't help Beth. She fretted all the while she made supper, wondering how Jeb was doing . . . if he was hurting bad . . . if he was lonesome . . . until she could stand it no longer. She picked up the telephone.

"Number, please," Jessica said.

"Hi, Jess. Please get me the McAllisters' place."

"Right away, Beth."

Liddy answered. "McAllisters'."

"Liddy, I just called to see if Cal had mentioned how Jeb is doing?"

"Beth. It's good to talk to you. Cal said he was doing pretty well when he left there.

And that Jeb was really appreciative of the work everyone had done. They finished up the roof today, but Cal is going back over tomorrow to help with the livestock, and Matt told him he'd be out to check on Jeb, too."

Beth breathed a sigh of relief. "Oh, good. I was worried that seeing to the livestock might be too much for Jeb."

"I understand. I'd be the same way. But he is going to mend, Beth." Liddy tried to assure her.

"I know." Suddenly, she felt like crying. "Thank you, Liddy. I'll let you go now." With that, she quickly put the earpiece back on the hook. She was sure Jeb was going to mend . . . but would he want her around when he did?

She tried to get her mind off of the guilt she still felt and suggested to the children that they make Jeb some cookies to send out with Matt the next day. She was sure Jeb and any of the men still working out there would appreciate them.

Cassie and Lucas helped, and before long they had a very messy kitchen and a whole crock full of sugar cookies for Jeb. Beth made a quick telephone call to Emma and asked if it would be all right for her to drop them by for Matt to take out to the ranch.

Emma made sure her husband was going out and came back on the line. "Matt said he will be glad to take them out, Beth. Things are pretty calm in town, and the sheriff has given him a lot of leeway to help out."

"That's really nice of him. And thank Matt for me. I'll bring the cookies by on my way to work. Did he say how Jeb was doing when he left?"

"He told me he thought he would be all right. He can't do too much with his arm in that sling, but at least it was his left one. He assured Matt and Cal that he would be just fine."

Beth breathed a sigh of relief as she told Emma good-bye and ended the call. Surely, if both Matt and Cal thought he'd be fine, she could stop worrying so.

She'd barely turned around when her telephone rang her ring . . . three short rings . . . a pause . . . and three more. She answered quickly, thinking it might be Darcie, as she'd already talked to Emma and Liddy, and those three were about the only people she talked to at home.

"Beth? Is that you?" Her heart dipped and dove down into her stomach at the sound of the masculine voice. It was Jeb. "Beth? Did I do this right?"

She finally found her voice. "Jeb . . . yes, it's me. You did fine."

"Good. I never used a telephone before. I wanted to thank you for getting it hooked up . . . and for —"

"You're welcome. Cassie and Lucas missed seeing you tonight."

"I missed them, too. I —"

"I know they would love to talk to you . . . let me get them."

It only took a minute for the children to get to the telephone. Not only were they excited to be hearing from Jeb, they'd never talked on the telephone before. Beth pulled a kitchen chair close for Lucas to climb onto so that he could reach the phone on the wall. He talked first, then Cassie.

"We made some cookies for you tonight, Uncle Jeb. Miss Beth thought they might make you feel better," Lucas said right off.

When it was her turn to talk, Cassie assured her uncle that they were both behaving for Beth. It was touching to hear each of them ask Jeb how he was feeling and when they would see him again.

From what Beth couldn't help but hear, Jeb asked about school and the upcoming Christmas program, and they each took a turn at telling him about their day. That they loved him was obvious. She knew they cared about her, but Jeb was family, a closer link to their papa, and they were looking forward to moving out to the ranch with him.

"Uncle Jeb wants to speak to you, Miss Beth," Cassie said, breaking into her thoughts.

"Thank you." Beth took the earpiece from her and held it to her ear. "I'm here, Jeb," she said into the mouthpiece. "How are you feeling?"

"Better since I talked to Cassie and Lucas. They're behaving for you?"

"Of course they are. They always do."

"Seems strange not to have seen them today," Jeb said.

"It did for them, too." *And for me.*

"I guess these telephones have their uses, don't they?"

"Yes, they do." Beth connected people every day in her work, but she'd never really appreciated the instrument at her fingertips until now.

Jeb chuckled. "Once you figure out how to use them. Took me a couple of tries 'til I got someone to say, 'Number, please.' And I did like Matt showed me and just told them who I wanted to talk to."

"You did just right."

"Well, thank you again for getting it hooked up for me while I was laid up."

228

"I'm glad they got to it before you got back out there." *I just wish you weren't there by yourself.* "You take care. Will you be able to make the Christmas program on Friday night? I'm sure Cal and Liddy would be glad to bring you in, if you're up to it. If not, I can bring the children out on Saturday, if you'd like me to."

"Oh, I'm planning on being there for that program. But I admit I didn't realize it was this week. I'll talk to Cal about it."

"Just let me know. And try not to overdo it, all right?"

"Don't worry 'bout me overdoing it. Not much I can do with this arm in splints and in this sling."

Beth was sure he'd be pushing himself as far as that arm would let him. "Liddy told me that Cal would be over to help you tomorrow. Try to let him, will you?"

"I'll try. Well, I guess I'd better let you go. You have to go to work tomorrow. If I can't get to town, I'll telephone tomorrow evening."

"I'll tell Cassie and Lucas. I know they felt better just hearing your voice tonight." And so did she.

"Good night, Beth."

"Good night, Jeb." Beth replaced the earpiece into the hook. *Thank You, Lord, for let-*

ting us hear from him. Please watch over him tonight, please heal him, and keep him safe. In Jesus' name, amen.

Jeb poured himself a cup of lukewarm coffee and eased himself into a chair at the table in the kitchen.

It had been so good to talk to Cassie and Lucas . . . and Beth. It wasn't anywhere near as good as talking to them in person, but it was better than nothing. He really missed them all tonight.

One thing the last few days had made crystal clear to him was that he was here to stay — no matter what happened between him and Beth.

He'd never been so touched in his life as he was when Doc pulled up in the yard today and he'd seen for himself just how this community had come together to help him in a way he'd never experienced before. He'd only briefly talked to some of these men at church, yet they'd shown their Christianity by caring enough to reach out a hand and help when he was in need. He wanted to be here to return the favor for any who might need him in the future, too.

It warmed his heart to know that it was Beth who first came up with the idea of getting help to finish the roof, as Cal and Matt told him. And they'd said they actually had to tell some people that they had enough help. This had become home.

He never really realized how lonely he'd been without family and close friends nearby . . . probably because he'd only been around other cowboys for so long. There were some good ones, but most were like him, moving place to place. It was hard to develop close friendships when no one stayed in the same place for long.

And John Biglow was a good man, but Jeb didn't really know him well enough to know if he was a Christian or not. Jeb had done the best he could to stay close to the Lord, reading his Bible and praying often, but he hadn't known what he'd been missing out on until he came to Roswell and became a part of a church family and a member of the community. He finally felt like he belonged somewhere.

Jeb took a sip from his cup. He should have heated it up. It had tasted better when it was fresh, but was still nowhere near as good as Beth's. Beth. What was he going to do about her? She'd sounded a little strained and distant tonight, but maybe it was just the way she sounded on the telephone. He'd wanted to thank her for her part in getting the roof finished and for all the help he had, but she kept changing the subject. He sighed and shook his head. He had a feeling she was still feeling bad and blaming herself for his fall. But it was his own fault. He knew better than to move quickly up on the roof. She'd just startled him with her accusations, and he hadn't watched what he was doing.

And she had looked so pretty while she was telling him off — even though she'd been so wrong about that letter and accused him of planning to leave. And to think, all he'd wanted was to get the house finished by that deadline she'd given him so he could ask her to marry him again!

He knew that the Lord led him here because of Harland's death, but Jeb believed that He had another purpose in bringing him to Roswell other than taking responsibility for Cassie and Lucas and making a home for them. He truly believed that the Lord had chosen Beth as his mate. Now, if he could just convince *her* of that fact.

He bowed his head and prayed for the Lord to show him the way.

CHAPTER 12

Beth didn't know who was more relieved after they talked to Jeb . . . she or the children. Lucas and Cassie seemed much happier for the rest of the evening and excited about the upcoming Christmas program now that they were hopeful their uncle would be able to attend. She sent them off to bed and finished cleaning up the kitchen, feeling much better herself. Just hearing Jeb's voice and knowing that he was all right had eased her mind a bit . . . at least about that. It also made her ever more aware of how quickly she'd become used to having him around and how very much she was missing him now.

It wasn't until Cassie and Lucas were fast asleep and Beth sat down at the kitchen table with a cup of tea that she considered how she was going to feel once the children moved out to the ranch. The roof was finished; the house was pretty much ready for them to move into.

She sighed deeply. It was going to be awfully lonely here without them. But, as much as she would miss Cassie and Lucas, she'd finally accepted that they needed to be with their uncle. And he needed them. He'd been without family for a long time, and, in the past few months, she'd witnessed a bonding between the three of them. She would be all right with their move to the ranch. Surely she would.

But she wasn't sure her heart would ever be all right again if Jeb couldn't forgive her for causing his fall. Oh, he'd said he was trying to finish the house to answer her challenge, but did that mean he cared enough to propose to her again? Besides, that had been before the fall. Beth shook her head. How could he want to marry her after the way she'd acted, climbing that ladder and yelling at him?

She could still see the confused look on his face as she'd accused him of planning on selling the ranch and the frustration as he'd yelled back telling her she was wrong — just before he'd fallen off the roof. Remembering the sound of Jeb hitting the ground, the sight of him lying there, not moving, Beth shuddered. She truly had thought he was dead.

Now all she really wanted was for him to forgive her for not believing in him the way she should have, believing what Harland had told her about him instead of what she was seeing with her own eyes, and causing him all kinds of pain and suffering. But she didn't deserve his forgiveness, and she certainly couldn't expect him to still care for her after the way she'd treated him.

Beth shook her head. She loved Jeb. Pure and simple. But she had to come to grips with the fact that, after the way she'd caused his fall, she would probably never have a life with him now.

Taking a sip of tea, Beth pulled her Bible close and began to read. It was only then that she realized what she needed to do was to go to the Lord in prayer. If He could forgive her, surely Jeb could, too — with the Lord's help.

She bowed her head and prayed. *Oh, dear Lord, thank You for letting Jeb be all right. Please watch over him through the night and ease his pain. Please forgive me for losing my temper and causing him to fall off the roof. And, please let Jeb forgive me, too, if it be Your will. In Jesus' name, amen.*

Finally, Beth felt some peace of mind as she sat in the quiet, knowing God heard her prayers. She got up and carried her cup to the sink. She would ask Jeb for his forgiveness when she could talk to him alone, then she would leave it all in the Lord's hands.

The next couple of days were a little tough for Jeb, but at least he could get around some. His limp was more pronounced from all the aches and pains he felt, but he continually thanked the Lord above that he hadn't been hurt worse. He figured he wasn't worth much otherwise, though. He hadn't been able to mount his horse to get into town to see the children, and, even though he'd talked to them on the telephone, it just wasn't as good as seeing them in person.

The beds he'd ordered had come in and were delivered on Thursday, and Jeb had set them up, with Cal's help. They'd dug through some of the boxes of the household items that Harland had brought with him in his move West and found some linens to put on them. He was thankful Beth had sent them out with him when he started work on the house so they would be there when he needed them. The worktable she'd pointed out to him that had the bins for flour had come in and fit just right in the kitchen. The place was beginning to feel like a home.

When Cal had suggested that the children move out after the Christmas program on Friday, Jeb quickly placed a telephone call to see if it would be all right with Beth.

"Of course it is, Jeb." She paused for a moment. "I'll have them ready to go. But it might take me a few days to get all of their things together."

Jeb could hear the sadness in her voice and knew that she was going to have a hard time giving Cassie and Lucas up, as he'd always known she would. The last thing he wanted to do was hurt Beth, and if he had anything to do with it, she wouldn't really be giving them up — at least not for long.

"That's fine. All they need right now is enough for the weekend. The house is ready. At least, near enough. I'd figured to move them out sometime next week, anyway. Maybe on Sunday I'll be up to bringing in the wagon and packing up the rest of their things."

"They're very excited about making the move out there."

Jeb had a feeling it took a lot for her to tell him as much. "I can't wait to have them here. I've missed them something terrible." He'd missed her, too. More than he truly realized he would. But now wasn't the time to tell her . . . not when she was in town and he was out here. No, that needed to be done in person, and he hoped to be able to see her very soon and convince her that he loved her.

"Jeb?"

"I'm here. I guess I was woolgathering." *About you . . . about us.*

"I'll have them ready to go after the Christmas program. They're going to be so excited that you'll be attending and that they'll be with you this weekend."

"Thank you, Beth."

"You're welcome."

Now here it was Friday afternoon, and Jeb couldn't wait until tonight, when he'd see them all at the Christmas program. Cal and Liddy were going to pick him up, and the children would be coming back with him. He'd see Beth and attempt to get a feel for how she would react to another proposal from him.

He remembered that he'd been about to tell her he loved her right before he fell. While he was laid up, he'd thought about her reaction to the letter from John Biglow over and over again. She'd been so upset about the possibility of him leaving, but had it only been because he would be taking the children with him or because she cared for him, too?

Jeb thought she felt something for him, the way her cheeks turned that pretty shade of pink when he sometimes caught her watching him with the children or when she glanced up to see him looking at her from across the table, the way she made his favorite meals and always made sure he had something to take back to the ranch with him. Maybe it was too soon to expect her to care. She might still be grieving over Harland.

So many little things she did for him made Jeb think she might really care for him. But did she? Or was it only wishful thinking on his part? He only hoped her acts of kindness were done for the same reason he brought her flowers and took her to Emma's on Saturday nights — because he loved her and wanted to make her happy.

Dear Lord, please help me to know. I love this woman with all my heart, and I want the two of us to make this house a home for Cassie and Lucas. Please guide me here, and let me know what to do. In Jesus' name, amen.

Beth found herself leaning on the Lord with all that was within her over the next few days. Her heart had dropped to her toes when Jeb called Thursday night, wanting the children to move out to the ranch. Oh, she'd known it was coming, and she'd told herself she would be all right, but deep down, she knew her house was going to feel awfully empty without Cassie and Lucas there or Jeb stopping by each day to see them.

She tried not to show them how sad she was just thinking about their move. They were so happy and excited that Jeb was coming in for the Christmas program and that they would finally be moving out to the ranch, she didn't want to put a damper on their joy.

After she'd talked to Jeb on Thursday evening, she had kept herself busy by making some sugar cookies for the program the next night, and she also baked a cake and more cookies to send out to the ranch with Jeb and the children.

Cassie had been reading her cookbook and helping with the cooking for some weeks now, and Beth knew that between her and Jeb, they wouldn't starve. But she sure was going to miss having suppers with them and sharing the evenings with them.

Now, as she sat at work on Friday, she tried not to dwell on how lonesome it was going to be at her house. But it wasn't easy to keep it off her mind.

Liddy telephoned while she was at work

and apologized for Cal's part in speeding up the children's move. "I know Cal meant no harm, and he feels real bad that you might be upset with him, Beth. He just said Jeb seemed so lonely out there that the suggestion to go ahead and move the children just slipped out."

"It's all right, Liddy. They would have been moving soon anyway. I knew that."

"You know this isn't the end of —"

Beth didn't want to even think about endings. "Liddy, I'm sorry . . . my switchboard is lighting up. I'll see you this evening, all right?"

"Yes, of course —"

Beth disconnected the line and put the pin in for Emma's Café. "Beth?"

"Yes, it's me, Em."

"Oh, good. I never know who I'm going to get. Matt just told me that the children will be going back out to the ranch with Jeb tonight. Are you all right with that?"

"I don't have much choice in it, Emma . . . but I'll adjust."

"Oh, Beth. It's all going to work out. I just know it is."

"Thank you. It will. And Jeb needs them with him, too. Don't worry about me. I'll be all right. Cal and Liddy's wagon is going to be pretty full tonight. Would you and

241

Matt mind picking me up?"

"Of course not. Are you sure —"

"I'll be fine, Em," Beth commented. And for the moment, she thought she would.

But by the time Cal and Liddy showed up with their children and Jeb to pick up Cassie and Lucas that evening, Beth wasn't so sure.

Everyone pitched in to help load the wagon with the food Beth had made for the ranch and the program and the personal items the children were taking to the ranch. By the time they all were settled back in the wagon, ready to leave, she was feeling pretty sad.

"I'll get the rest of their things packed up tomorrow so you can pick them up on Sunday," she said to Jeb.

"Thank you, Beth. You're going to the program with us, aren't you?"

"I'll be there. But I figured Cal's and Liddy's wagon would be plumb full, so I asked Matt and Emma to pick me up. They'll be here anytime now."

For the first time, the children showed a little hesitancy about leaving her.

"You are coming, aren't you, Miss Beth?" Lucas asked.

Beth forced herself to smile and nod. "Of course I am. I wouldn't miss it. You save me a seat, all right?"

"We have room for you now, Beth." Jeb patted the empty space beside him.

"That's all right. I already asked Em and Matt. I'll be there soon."

Beth pulled her overcoat closer around her and watched the wagon full of people she loved head toward the school. Her eyes filled with tears, and she blinked them away quickly as Matt and Emma showed up. Em watched her closely but didn't say anything as Beth stepped up into the wagon and greeted Mandy.

When they arrived at the school, it was to find that the children had been gathered behind a curtain that had been strung up in front of the platform stage some of the men had put up.

Liddy had put her dessert, along with Beth's, on a table in back of the room, and Emma hurried off to add hers to the rest.

Jeb and the McAllisters had indeed saved them all a seat. Beth's just happened to be between Jeb and Liddy, and Jeb stood to let her sit down. In order to accommodate his broken arm, she had to turn slightly toward him, and she was flooded with guilt all over again at seeing his arm in that sling.

Matt and Emma sat in the row behind them, and it took a few minutes for everyone to get settled before the program began. Once the curtain opened, the audience clapped wildly, letting their little ones know how proud of them they were.

A large Christmas tree had been put up at the back of the stage, and it was beautiful, decorated with things all the children had brought from home. The popcorn garland that Jeb had helped the children string had been added to several others and, intertwined with the cranberry ones, looked very pretty. Homemade ornaments cut from paper or made from lace and ribbon hung all over the tree.

Beth quickly spotted Cassie on the back row of steps, while Lucas stood on the first. They'd been a little nervous about performing in front of so many people, and she sent up a silent prayer, asking for the Lord to give them the confidence they needed.

And He did. As they began to sing, her heart expanded in love for them. Their sweet faces intent on remembering the words and their young voices harmonizing together, they sang "O Come All Ye Faithful" and then "Joy to the World."

She spotted Grace and Amy, too, and knew Liddy was feeling the same way about her girls. Trying not to be obvious, she glimpsed at Jeb out of the corner of her eye and found that he appeared every bit as proud as she felt. The audience was asked to join in singing several Christmas carols, and the sound of so many voices singing "It Came Upon a Midnight Clear" and "Silent Night" had Beth's spine tingling.

Minister Turley ended the program by reading the story of Christ's birth from the book of Luke. And a night that had started out on a down note for Beth ended on one of thankfulness for the Savior who'd come to earth.

Thunderous applause erupted when the curtain was closed and opened again . . . all the children taking a bow. Beth tried not to think of telling Cassie and Lucas good-bye; instead, she busied herself behind the dessert table giving out treats.

When it was time for the children to go, Beth swallowed around the clump of unshed tears in her throat and gave them each a hug, promising to see them on Sunday.

Sunday could come none too soon for Beth. By the time Saturday evening rolled around, she wished she'd been working. It didn't take anywhere near as long as she'd thought it would to pack up the rest of Lucas's and Cassie's things, and by that afternoon she was more than a little lonesome.

She kept busy, cleaning house and baking bread to send with Jeb and the children. Emma was thoughtful and invited her over for supper that night, and Beth was glad for the company but felt out of sorts that Jeb and the children weren't with her. It was going to take some getting used to, this being alone again.

After coming home to a house that seemed emptier than ever, Beth could stand it no longer, and she placed a call to the ranch. It took several rings before he picked up on his end.

"Winslow Ranch."

"Jeb? It's Beth." Now that she was talking to him, she felt a little silly.

"You sound a little funny. Is everything all right?"

"Yes, of course." *I just miss you all.* "I . . . I just wanted to see how Lucas and Cassie and you are all doing."

"We're making supper. I'm trying my hand at pancakes. Cassie told me I have to let them bubble up before turning them over. You should have seen the mess I made of the few I flipped too soon."

Beth chuckled just thinking about it, and she wished she had been there to witness him flipping those cakes.

"Cassie and Lucas helped me unpack

246

some of those boxes of household things of Harland's that you sent out here," Jeb continued. "Cassie has this kitchen in good working order, and Lucas has been a big help outside in the barn."

They were such good children. "I'm glad they have been able to lend a hand to you."

"I'm just glad they're here. But I guess you're missing them, too."

"Yes, well, I'll get used to it." *Oh, dear Lord, please let me get used to it.* "I'll let you get back to your meal, and I'll see you all tomorrow at church." Beth didn't wait for Jeb to say anything else. She couldn't trust her voice to stay steady.

Sunday morning, Beth was up early. She put on a pot roast to cook while she was at church. She'd meant to ask Jeb and the children to come over for Sunday dinner when she'd talked to him the night before, but she'd been so flustered and emotional talking to him she'd forgotten. She would ask them at church, and if he declined her invitation, well then, she'd have her supper for several days.

She dressed in her best dress and took care with her hair. It was a beautiful day, with Christmas only a week away. She'd been knitting at night for some time now, making mufflers for both Cassie and Lucas, but she wanted to buy them something else. She needed to talk to Jeb and see if he'd decided what he was getting them.

With the prospect of seeing them all again, her heart felt a bit lighter than the day before. Beth chuckled and shook her head. She was pitiful. It had only been one whole day since she had seen them. She'd just put on her cloak and started out the door when Jeb pulled his wagon up.

"We were hoping we'd catch you. I'm still not used to having that telephone, or I would have placed a call to you to see if you wanted to ride to church with us." Jeb grinned at her. "It only dawned on me that I could have when we got to town."

"Yes, Miss Beth, we want you to come with us," Cassie said.

"We love it at the ranch, but we've missed you," Lucas added.

"I've missed you, too. And thank you. A ride would be nice." Beth climbed up onto the seat and sat down beside Jeb. He looked a little awkward holding the reins in only one hand, and guilt flooded her once more. "Would you like me to take the reins?"

"Thank you, but I'm fine. Got to handle it for the next month or so. Cassie and Lucas hitched up the wagon for me, and thankfully, my team is easy to handle."

Much as she would miss them, Beth was glad the children were able to help Jeb. When they arrived at church, Cassie and Lucas hurried out of the wagon and over to talk with the McAllisters' children. Beth didn't know when she might have the chance to talk to Jeb alone again.

Realizing it might be only for a minute, the words she'd been waiting to say tumbled out of her mouth. "Jeb, I am so sorry for causing you to fall. Can you ever forgive me?"

"Beth, I told you it wasn't your fault. There is nothing to forgive."

"Oh, yes, there is. I yelled at you. I was awful that day."

Jeb grinned at her and shook his head. "You had reasons. But if it will make you feel better, then I forgive you for yelling — but it still wasn't your fault that I fell."

"Thank you," Beth responded simply.

Jeb crooked his good arm and Beth took it, feeling as if a huge weight lifted off her shoulders. He might never ask her to marry him again, but he forgave her.

As they strolled into church together, the joy Beth felt in knowing that Jeb had forgiven her lasted well past the worship service and throughout the day, as Jeb and the children came back to the house and took dinner with her. She loved being in their company.

It was only when it was time for them to leave that Beth's joy turned bittersweet. She truly was glad they were happy at the ranch with Jeb. She just wished she was going back there with them, instead of staying in the emptiest house in town.

Jeb couldn't get the sight of Beth waving good-bye to them out of his mind. She'd seemed so alone and forlorn, and the children didn't look too happy about leaving her there, either. Maybe he should have waited until after Christmas to move them to the ranch.

When Liddy and Cal stopped by on their way back from town on Monday and asked if Cassie and Lucas could go home with them for the afternoon, Jeb realized he had the opportunity he'd been waiting for. He was determined that he wasn't going to wait any longer to tell Beth how he felt about her and that it was time to deal with the challenge she'd given him. He'd given her more than one chance to bring up the subject, and she hadn't done it. Well, he was going to bring it up himself. The house was finished, and he was about to propose to

Miss Beth Morgan again, and this time it was for real.

"Sure. I need to go into town and pick up a few things. Cal, think you could help me get my wagon hitched up?"

"Sure can." It took only a few minutes, and Jeb was on the wagon seat ready to take off in the opposite direction. "I'll come by and get Cassie and Lucas when I return."

"Well, plan on staying for supper, you hear?" Liddy suggested.

Jeb grinned. "Thank you, Liddy. I'll look forward to it."

"Bye, Uncle Jeb," Lucas yelled from the back of the wagon.

"If you see Miss Beth, tell her we said hello," Cassie called to him.

Jeb nodded and waved back. He'd tell her. Because the main reason he was going into town was to see Beth. She'd given him a challenge, and he'd met it. It was time for her to make a decision.

Beth's switchboard had been busy all day. It seemed everyone in town wanted to know if the children were happy at the ranch or if she was missing them. Or when she would be seeing them again.

"Well, what are you going to do about Christmas, Beth?" Alma asked.

251

"I don't know just yet, Mrs. Alma. But I have plenty of friends. I'm sure I won't be alone."

"Well, if you want my opinion, you ought to . . ."

Beth's switchboard began to light up again. "Hold on, Mrs. Alma." She pulled the pin on the Pauly Hotel's socket. "Number, please?"

"Get me the sheriff's office, will you please, Beth?" Mr. Williams, the hotel manager, asked.

"Right away." As she reached to insert the hotel's pin into the sheriff's socket, she placed another pin into Doc Bradshaw's office socket. "Number, please?"

"Beth, it's Myrtle —"

"Beth?" It was Jeb's voice, but she hadn't connected his line, had she? "I need to talk to you."

She glanced at her switchboard, but his line wasn't lit up.

"Beth?"

Beth turned in her chair and saw him standing just inside the telephone office door. She jumped up, dropping the unconnected end of the lines she'd been holding onto the switchboard. "Jeb, what's wrong? Are the children all right?"

"They're fine. I came to talk to you."

Beth brought a hand to her chest. "Oh . . . I thought . . . but I'm working."

Jeb crossed the room quickly, his limp barely noticeable.

Her pulse began to race, and she placed a palm over her rapidly beating heart.

Jeb stood only inches away, looking deep into her eyes. "I told you I was going to ask you again once the house was done. Well, it's done and you need to make up your mind."

"Jeb, I —" Beth's heartbeat sounded like thunder in her ears, and she wondered if Darcie could hear it. She'd never felt so flustered in her life. She knew she needed to be doing something . . . she was at work. She turned around and found Darcie watching the two of them, several lines in her hand waiting to be plugged into sockets. "Can this wait? I'm working. I —"

"I've waited long enough." Jeb pulled her close with his good arm. "I need an answer now."

Now. He needed an answer.

Beth looked back to see her switchboard lighting up all over the place, and Darcie trying to take care of both switchboards while trying not to miss a thing going on in the office. For the first time since she'd come to work here, Beth decided some things were just more important than the Roswell Telephone and Manufacturing Company.

"An answer to what?"

"You told me that if I finished the house by Christmas, you just might marry me. Back then, when I asked you to marry me, we barely knew each other and it was for the children's sake. This time I'm asking simply because I love you . . . with all my heart, and I can't imagine not seeing you every day. I want you out at the ranch with me and Cassie and Lucas. I know you may never love me like you loved Harland, but, Beth, will you please marry me?"

It suddenly didn't matter if the whole town would soon know what went on here. She turned her undivided attention to the man she loved. "Oh, Jeb! I . . . you . . ."

Beth stopped and took a deep breath. She had to tell him everything. "I thought I could learn to love Harland. I truly did. But I'd been having second thoughts about marrying him for weeks before he died. I was going to tell him the next time he came into town, only I didn't have a chance before he was killed in the stampede. I promised myself that I would never marry a man I didn't know and didn't love after that. Then you came into my life, and I've felt so guilty

over the growing feelings I've had for you. I
—"

Jeb shushed her with a finger at her lips. "I understand. I've had my share of guilt over falling in love with you. But I have. Deeply and completely. And I want nothing more than to marry you, if you'll have me —"

Beth's heart seemed to have wings as it rapidly beat in her chest. "Oh, Jeb. You are the only man I've truly loved . . . and yes, oh yes, I *will* marry you."

Beth tried to be careful of his bad arm and sore ribs as Jeb pulled her closer and bent his head toward her. Their lips met and clung in a kiss that turned the challenge of a moment into a promise of a lifetime.

EPILOGUE

Christmas morning dawned bright and cold, but Jeb didn't feel it as he hurried downstairs to stir the coals in the fireplaces to life and add logs to them. The warmth he felt generated from the love in his heart . . . for his new wife and the niece and nephew they would raise together.

He had little time to think about it, however, as Cassie and Lucas rushed downstairs.

"Merry Christmas, Uncle Jeb!" Lucas shouted.

"Yes, Merry Christmas," Cassie called from behind him.

"Merry Christmas! I'm sorry we don't have a tree this Christmas," Jeb apologized. "Next year, I'll go with Cal to cut a great big one."

"It's all right, Uncle Jeb," Lucas assured him. "We have what we wanted."

"Yes, we do," Cassie agreed. "We've been

praying that all that courting you were doing worked and that Miss — that *Aunt* Beth would agree to marry you so we could all live here on the ranch together."

Jeb laughed and nodded. "Well, I sure am glad the Lord heard those prayers. I surely am. Because that was my Christmas wish, also." He gave them each a one-armed hug. "I do believe, even though we don't have a tree up, there are a few other gifts for you in the back parlor. You go ahead, and I'll go get your aunt Beth."

The children rushed off, and he went to look for his new wife. He still couldn't believe that Beth had accepted his proposal and agreed to marry him on Christmas Eve . . . much less that they actually had been married the night before, with half the town as witnesses and a wonderful reception following at Emma's Café.

To thank their best friends for all they'd done to help them prepare for such a rushed wedding right on Christmas Eve, Beth had insisted that the McAllisters and the Johnsons come out to the ranch for Christmas dinner after church. It's what she wanted . . . and no one could tell her no, least of all him.

Beth had come down earlier, and now he found her in the kitchen, just closing the oven door on the huge turkey she'd put in to roast while they were at church. Jeb leaned against the door frame, thoroughly enjoying the chance to watch his new bride putter around, until she finally turned and spotted him.

The delicate color that stole up her cheeks and the sweet smile she gave him when she saw him were enough to warm him clear through.

"Jeb! I didn't hear you come downstairs. Coffee will be ready soon."

"I should have known you'd be down here with this stove. It's the real reason you accepted my proposal, isn't it?" he teased.

Beth giggled. "Well, I'll admit, my fingers have been itching to cook a meal on it ever since I found out you bought it. But it's certainly not the reason I married you."

Jeb crossed the room in two strides and pulled her close with his good arm. "No?"

She shook her head as she gazed into his eyes. "No. I married you because I do love you, Jeb . . . more than I ever thought possible."

Jeb's heart seemed to expand in his chest. He knew she loved him, as he did her. They'd told each other so over and over in the past few days. But he'd never tire of hearing it . . . nor of saying it. "I love you, Beth."

Jeb bent his head and captured her lips in a kiss meant to assure her completely that he was telling the truth. Cassie and Lucas yelled for them to hurry, and Beth quickly broke the kiss and pulled away.

"We're coming," Jeb answered. But he caught Beth's arm as she started out of the kitchen and pulled her back into his embrace. The children could wait another minute or two.

"Merry Christmas," he whispered right before his lips claimed Beth's once more in a lingering kiss.

"Uncle Jeb, Aunt Beth!" Lucas was getting impatient to open his presents.

Jeb chuckled as Beth broke the kiss and pulled him toward the parlor. He followed willingly, thanking the Lord above for leading him to Beth . . . and to a place called home.

Dear Readers,

While I've lived all over the South, and we have just moved from Mississippi to Oklahoma — my husband's home state — New Mexico will always be special. I was born and raised there, and it's where my deep faith in the Lord and my Christian walk began and grew.

When the idea for *A Promise Made* came to me, I knew right where I wanted to set it — in my home town of Roswell, NM. After delving deeper into the town's history, the scenes of my story began to form. When the characters seemed to come alive to me, one story lead to another as *A Place Called Home* and *Making Amends* also took shape, with the Lord's help.

I hope you enjoy New Mexico and Emma's story as she strives to keep a promise, Beth's as she fights with giving up the children she's come to love as her own, and finally, Darcie's story, as she struggles with letting go of pain from the past and learns to forgive. As in our own lives, it's only with the Lord's help that they are able to find the way to true happiness.

Trusting in Him always,
Janet Lee Barton

The employees of Thorndike Press hope you have enjoyed this Large Print book. All our Thorndike and Wheeler Large Print titles are designed for easy reading, and all our books are made to last. Other Thorndike Press Large Print books are available at your library, through selected bookstores, or directly from us.

For information about titles, please call:
    (800) 223-1244

or visit our Web site at:
    http://gale.cengage.com/thorndike

To share your comments, please write:
    Publisher
    Thorndike Press
    295 Kennedy Memorial Drive
    Waterville, ME 04901